Best Friend's Girl

<u>"Saved by the Bell" titles include:</u>

Mark-Paul Gosselaar: Ultimate Gold
Mario Lopez: High-Voltage Star
Behind the Scenes at "Saved by the Bell"
Beauty and Fitness with "Saved by the Bell"
Dustin Diamond: Teen Star
The "Saved by the Bell" Date Book

<u>Hot new fiction titles:</u>

#1   Bayside Madness
#2   Zack Strikes Back
#3   California Scheming
#4   Girls' Night Out
#5   Zack's Last Scam
#6   Class Trip Chaos
#7   That Old Zack Magic
#8   Impeach Screech!
#9   One Wild Weekend
#10   Kelly's Hero
#11   Don't Tell a Soul
#12   Computer Confusion
#13   Silver Spurs
#14   Best Friend's Girl
#15   Zack in Action
#16   Operation: Clean Sweep

Best Friend's Girl

by Beth Cruise

Collier Books
Macmillan Publishing Company
New York
Maxwell Macmillan Canada
Toronto
Maxwell Macmillan International
New York   Oxford   Singapore   Sydney

Collier Books
Macmillan Publishing Company
866 Third Avenue
New York, NY 10022

Maxwell Macmillan Canada, Inc.
1200 Eglinton Avenue East
Suite 200
Don Mills, Ontario M3C 3N1

Macmillan Publishing Company is part of the Maxwell Communication
Group of Companies.
First Collier Books edition 1994
Printed in the United States of America
10 9 8 7 6 5 4 3 2

Library of Congress Cataloging-in-Publication Data

Cruise, Beth.
    Best friend's girl / by Beth Cruise.—1st Collier Books ed.
        p. cm.
    Summary: Slater and Kelly begin a tentative romance when their
feelings for Jessie and Zack change.
    ISBN 0-02-042786-7
    [1. High schools—Fiction.   2. Schools—Fiction.]   I. Title.
PZ7.C88827Be   1994
[Fic]—dc20   94-11670

**To all the
"Saved by the Bell" fans
who have ever been struck
by Cupid's arrow**

Chapter 1

▲ ▼ ▲ ▼ ▲

Zack Morris leaned back against the stone steps of Bayside High. A warm breeze stirred his blond hair as he looked up at a clear blue sky. He turned to inspect the mellow brick of the school, and gave a heavy sigh.

"Help me out, Screech," he said to his friend. "You got an *A* in algebra. I can't figure out this equation. If the value of *A* is perfect beach weather and the value of *B* is Saturday morning, how do you come up with *C*, school?"

"That's easy, Zack," Samuel "Screech" Powers said in the high-pitched voice that had earned him his nickname. "It's School Cleanup Day at Bayside High. And you volunteered to be here."

"Pinch me," Zack declared, a sparkle in his hazel eyes. "I must be dreaming. What was I thinking?"

"You weren't thinking at all," Lisa Turtle said as she adjusted her sun hat to the perfect angle. "You saw Kelly volunteer, so you raised your hand."

Zack smiled at the mention of his girlfriend. It was true. He had been looking at Kelly Kapowski's beautiful deep blue eyes and perfect cheerleader legs when he raised his hand. Things between them had cooled off lately, and he wasn't sure why. He'd do anything to gain points with his gorgeous girlfriend.

"Where *is* Kelly?" he wondered aloud. "When I called to tell her I'd pick her up, she said she was on her way out the door already. She should have been here before me."

Lisa shrugged. "Maybe she stopped at the Max for a glass of juice."

"Is she growing the oranges, too?" Zack complained.

"Here she comes," Screech announced, shading his eyes with his hand. "And she's with Slater and Jessie."

Zack looked down the school walk and saw Kelly heading their way with A. C. Slater, his best friend. Slater was dressed in shorts and a navy tank shirt, and Zack stifled a moan. It wasn't easy being buddies with a guy who worked out so much. Slater probably had perfect muscle tone in his *eyebrows*.

Walking at Slater's side was one of Zack's other best friends, Jessie Spano. Jessie's long legs easily kept pace with Slater's energetic stride. Jessie was Slater's on-again, off-again girlfriend. These days the gang wasn't sure whether they were on or off. Jessie assumed they were *on*. But Zack was beginning to wonder if Slater had other ideas.

There was a scowl on Slater's face instead of his usual easygoing grin. Zack guessed that Slater was just as cranky as he was to be spending a sunny Saturday at Bayside High.

"Look who I bumped into this morning at the beach," Jessie said as the threesome came up. "I went for an early morning swim, and there they were, sharing a box of doughnuts. They *say* they weren't going to play hooky, but it's probably a good thing I showed up." Jessie grinned teasingly, tossing her long brown curls.

"I guess all three of us had the same idea," Kelly said brightly. "Get in a nice bracing swim before slaving away here."

"Besides, Jess, you can't play hooky if there's no school," Slater pointed out brusquely. "Kelly and I weren't going to ditch you guys."

"I was just kidding," Jessie said, her hazel eyes clouding over. It seemed like everything she said to Slater came out wrong these days.

Slater saw the hurt in Jessie's eyes. "I know," he said gently. "I didn't mean to jump down your throat, Jessie. I guess I'm just in a bad mood."

"Who isn't," Zack agreed gloomily. "This is the first time I've volunteered for something that didn't get me out of class. If this is what it's like, I'm going to sit on my hands from now on."

"Well, we'd better head to the gym," Kelly said. "Mr. Belding said he's going to hand out the cleanup assignments promptly at ten o'clock."

"And the sooner we get started, the sooner we can leave," Zack added, standing up.

"And the sooner we can go to the beach," Kelly said. "I never did get my swim this morning."

"I'm heading for the mall," Lisa said. "There's a half-price sale at my favorite store." Lisa was clothes crazy. She considered a multivitamin plus a trip to the mall a necessary part of each day.

"The gym for me," Slater said. "I need a workout."

"You need a workout like a turtle needs a shell," Zack grumbled good-naturedly.

"Speaking of turtles, I've got to get to the aquarium," Screech said. "My favorite sea turtle, Seymour, is due to have a little turtlet any second."

"*Seymour*, Screech?" Zack asked pointedly as he swung open the door of Bayside High.

Screech scratched his frizzy curls. "Oh. Good point, Zack. I guess Seymour is a guy turtle. Maybe he's just getting fat. Do you think I've been feeding him too much peanut butter?"

Lisa rolled her eyes. "Why don't you ask him, Screech?"

"That's silly, Lisa," Screech said as he loped beside her in his size-eleven orange high-top sneakers. "Seymour can't talk."

"I know that, Screech," Lisa said patiently.

"Especially with all that peanut butter in his mouth," Screech concluded.

▲　▼　▲

A few minutes later, Zack slumped back against the bleachers while he waved an impatient hand in the air. "Mr. Belding? It's ten-fifteen," he called out. "Can't we get started?"

"We're losing prime time for rays," Daisy Tyler pouted.

"And we're getting a very tardy start," Binky Tolliver put in, pushing his glasses up on his nose.

Mr. Belding nervously surveyed the few rows of students. He looked at his watch. "I thought I'd give everyone just a little more time to get here. Another five minutes."

"Mr. B., I hate to break it to you," Slater said. "But I think this is it."

"But it's such a low turnout," Mr. Belding said, frowning. "I don't understand. Everyone was so enthusiastic when I brought up the idea of School Cleanup Day at assembly. We all agreed to help Mr. Monza out with the new recycling laws."

"Mr. B., what day was assembly?" Zack asked.

"Friday," Mr. Belding said.

"And what *time* was assembly?" Zack persisted.

Mr. Belding frowned, trying to remember. "Well, it was last period. And it was right after I announced that Mr. Monza would be out for a couple of weeks since his wife had twins. Then we took up that collection for diapers . . . So I guess it was about . . . two-twenty?"

"My point exactly," Zack said. "As soon as you finished talking, assembly would be over. We could all go home. You could have asked if anyone wanted to lick the gym floor clean with their *tongues*, and everyone would have raised their hands."

"I think this is the best you're going to do, Mr. B.," Kelly said sympathetically.

"I see your point, gang," Mr. Belding said dryly. "Oh, well. Then I guess we'd better get started." He looked down at his clipboard. "Okay, the first job is to box up all the old lost and found items so we can donate them to charity. They're in the back of the utility closet in the basement. And while you're there, you might as well sweep it out."

"Ewwww, spiders," Lisa whispered.

"I've *seen* that closet," Zack murmured. "I swear there's an old chemistry professor buried back there."

Slater raised his hand, and Kelly's followed.

"Very good, A. C., Kelly," Mr. Belding said, making a note. "Okay, the next project is to wash the graffiti off the north fence of the school. It's a disgrace. And besides, I do *not* appreciate being called Mr. Smell-ding."

"That job could take all day," Greg Tolan murmured behind them.

"And it's all the way on the other side of the practice field," Zack observed. "It's practically Siberia."

"And it's so far from the cafeteria," Phyllis Ptowski said.

Kelly raised her hand, and Slater's shot up a second later.

"My, my, you two are enthusiastic," Mr. Belding said, making another note. "Now I have a good one here. Who wants to sort and box the old books the library is donating to the homeless shelter?"

"Bor-ing," Will Cruikshank said.

"I'm allergic to dust," Zack said.

"Come on," Mr. Belding said. "The library is so cozy."

"And lonesome," Lisa shivered. "Who would come by to see me? I'd be all alone up there."

Kelly and Slater raised their hands.

Mr. Belding lowered his clipboard. "Now, wait a second here. Kelly and A.C. can't do *every-thing*. So far I only have the two of them down on my list."

"Too bad they're not in love," Lisa said with a giggle. "It's practically romantic."

Jessie laughed. "They vant to be alone," she said in a fake deep voice.

Slater and Kelly exchanged guilty looks. Kelly quickly looked away. Lisa and Jessie didn't realize how close they were to the truth.

Kelly wasn't in love with Slater. But she *was* interested. And he was interested in her, too. Even though their relationships with Zack and Jessie were on the rocks, they weren't sure what to do next.

When the gang had spent a long weekend in Santa Fe, things had changed between Kelly and Slater. He'd always been her friend, but suddenly there was the possibility of romance. For the first time, Kelly had realized that she had practically nothing in common with Zack. And she had *everything* in common with Slater.

They both were crazy about sports and were totally active. They both loved to dance. They loved horror movies and ice-cream sundaes. And they both were generally happy with their lives. Zack and Jessie were always running around trying to change things. Zack was bored when things went smoothly, day after day. And Jessie was always looking for a cause that needed her.

Once they had compared notes, she and Slater had discovered that they were tired of running after Zack and Jessie. They were tired of being in relationships where all they did was worry and argue.

But Kelly knew that her attraction for Slater went deeper than just having things in common.

She had glimpsed a sensitive side to him in Santa Fe, and she wanted to know more about it.

So far they'd only shared one kiss. And they might never get a chance to share another, Kelly thought in frustration. Ever since they'd returned to Palisades, they hadn't had a chance to be alone. There were always parties and games and get-togethers. And whenever they had thought they could steal some time by themselves, somebody else from the gang had wanted to tag along. Even this morning at the beach, they had just begun to talk when Jessie had shown up.

Slater gave her a shrug, and she smiled ruefully. How could they find out if they really were compatible if they never got a chance to be alone?

"Okay, that's it," Mr. Belding said, slapping his clipboard against his leg in frustration. "I'm just going to have to assign tasks. Slater and Kelly, you can pick up the trash on the football field, since Slater's the quarterback and Kelly's head cheerleader. Don't forget to separate out cans for recycling."

Kelly tried not to look pleased. Slater turned his smile into a frown. Together, they listened to Mr. Belding divide the other tasks of the day.

"Well, kids," Mr. Belding said when he'd finished. "Thank you for coming. Do your best, and

I'll be making the rounds to make sure you don't have any problems. There are work gloves and recycling bags by the door."

Zack turned to Slater. "I saw how disappointed you were, buddy. If you want, I'll switch with you. I scored an easy cleanup. I just have to box up unused cans of food in the cafeteria and recycle the used ones."

"Thanks, but no thanks, Morris. No way I'm spending my morning in the kitchen," Slater said.

"Kelly, I'd be happy to switch with you," Jessie said as she drew her long hair back in a ponytail. "I'm supposed to help Zack."

"That's okay, Jessie," Kelly said. "You're *so* much better at recycling than I am."

"Well, I guess you're stuck with Slater, then," Zack said. "Try not to miss me too much."

Kelly blushed and turned away. "I'll do my best, Zack," she said.

"Don't do anything I wouldn't do," Jessie called merrily to Slater.

Slater winced. But after Jessie and Zack had walked off, he turned to Kelly and grinned.

"Alone at last," he said.

"How romantic," Kelly said teasingly, grinning back at him. "Just you, me, and the garbage!"

Chapter 2

▲ ▼ ▲ ▼ ▲

Zack held up a can. "Lima beans," he said. "Why would Ms. Meadows order ten cases of lima beans? I don't know anybody who likes lima beans. Even *Slater* doesn't like them, and he'll eat anything."

"She didn't order them," Jessie said as she tossed an empty can into a recycling bag. "She ordered ten cases of *black* beans for her enchilada pie."

"I love that enchilada pie," Zack said.

"But the company wouldn't take the lima beans back, so finally Ms. Meadows decided it was taking more time and energy to argue with them than it would to just donate the cans to a charity."

Zack placed the can in the carton he was filling. "I'm just grateful she won't be making enchilada pie with lima beans," he said. "That would rate a ten on the yuck-o-meter."

"Ms. Meadows wouldn't do that," Jessie said. "You know how meticulous she is about her recipes. Bayside is incredibly lucky to have such a good cook. I tasted the food at Valley High once. Talk about the yuck-o-meter! This meal would have broken the scale."

"I have to admit I was wrong and you were right," Zack said. "When Mr. Belding hired a cook who ran a health food store, I was scared. I thought for sure there was a major tofu tundra in my future."

Jessie paused, holding an empty milk jug. "Excuse me. Is this Zack Morris talking?" she asked teasingly. "Wait, it can't be. You just admitted you were *wrong* about something."

Zack looked sheepish. "I admit I'm wrong all the time. Well, some of the time. All right, once in a while."

"When a deep freeze comes to Palisades," Jessie said. "What's that . . . about every ten years?"

Zack rocked back on his heels. "You sound like Kelly, Jessie."

"I consider that a compliment," Jessie said. "Kelly has your number, all right." Jessie tossed another milk jug in the PLASTICS container.

"These days she thinks I'm a jerk," Zack said.

"If the sneaker fits . . . ," Jessie said. "But don't let it bother you. I'm walking around in the same shoes with Slater. I never admit I'm wrong, either. It drives Slater crazy."

"I drive Kelly crazy, too," Zack said, easing himself up on the bench against the wall. "No wonder she's been so weird lately. I never really apologized for that scam I tried to pull in Santa Fe. I guess I thought if I didn't bring up imper-sonating Daredevil Dave Laramie, she'd forget all about it. Pretty stupid, huh?"

"No stupider than me never apologizing for neglecting Slater that weekend," Jessie said with a sigh. She flopped down next to Zack on the bench. "I was so busy trying to prove to my moth-er that her boyfriend was a big bad criminal that I totally ignored Slater. Then when the whole thing blew up in my face, I justified myself all over the place. No wonder he's been giving me the cold shoulder."

Zack and Jessie gloomily put their chins in their hands.

"We pushed them too far this time," Zack said.

"We did," Jessie agreed.

"And we don't deserve them."

"You're right," Jessie said. "But they love us, anyway."

"Yeah, and we're very lucky for that," Zack said, jumping up. "Let's apologize to them. Right now."

"Now?" Jessie asked. "We're supposed to be working. What if Mr. Belding comes by?"

"We'll say we went to get a soda or something," Zack said. "We're *volunteers*, remember? How much trouble can we get into? Besides, I can't work when I'm worried. I'll end up recycling full cans of lima beans and donating empty black-bean cans to the homeless shelter."

"Okay, I get your point," Jessie agreed. "Let's go."

▲   ▼   ▲

In the administration offices, Lisa's head popped over a desk. She waved a piece of paper in the air.

"Look at this, Screech," she called. "It's a freshman schedule from nineteen seventy-nine. Miss Mazursky has a whole box of schedules from practically the Stone Age underneath her desk. And they're always telling *us* to be organized!"

Lisa blew emphatically on the schedule to clear it of dust, and then started to cough.

"Just wait until we're their age," Screech said. "We'll be able to do whatever we want. I'll be able to keep as many back issues of *Science Gazette* as I want in my locker. But wait. I probably won't have a school locker by then. I'll be an adult. Where will I keep those back issues of *Science Gazette*? My mom doesn't want them in my closet."

Lisa tried to speak, but she just kept on coughing.

"Are you okay?" Screech asked, bending down over her. He adored Lisa. She was the love of his life, even though *he* got on *her* nerves.

Screech whacked her on the back, and she shot forward toward the carton of schedules, inhaling more dust. She coughed even more.

"Oops, sorry. Lisa? Lisa?"

Lisa shot him a malevolent look between coughs.

"Mr. Belding has a water dispenser in his

office," Screech said helpfully. "I'll get you a glass."

"Don't . . . bother," Lisa croaked. If Screech fetched her a glass of water, it would probably get spilled all over her fresh pink corduroy overalls.

Still coughing, Lisa headed for Mr. Belding's office. Screech went back to tying up bundles of papers with twine. Suddenly he heard a scream from Mr. Belding's office.

"Lisa!" Screech called. There was no answer.

Lisa was in trouble! Screech sprang to his feet and rushed toward Mr. Belding's office, only to trip over his stack of papers and go flying. His feet got tangled up in the twine, and he tried to kick it away. But the twine only got more wound around his ankles as he squirmed. Screech crawled and wriggled his way to Mr. Belding's office door.

He threw himself flat across the threshold and twisted his head around frantically. "Lisa?" he gasped.

"What?" Lisa asked. She turned and looked down at him. A few drops of water slid off the glass she was holding and dripped on his nose. "Are you okay, Screech?"

"I heard you scream."

"I know," Lisa sighed. "Isn't it divine?"

"The scream?" Screech asked as he struggled

to free himself of the twine. "I thought it was kind of scary."

"No. The Origami," Lisa explained.

"The what?"

Screech stood up and followed Lisa's gaze toward Mr. Belding's open closet door. An unzipped garment bag hung on a hook. Screech glimpsed the shimmer of satin material.

"I was looking for a glass, so I opened the closet door," Lisa explained. "After I got my water, I couldn't resist unzipping the bag."

"Gosh, Lisa," Screech said. "Isn't a garment bag kind of private property?"

Lisa shot him a scornful look. "For me, never. If it has to do with clothing, I've got to see it."

Screech took another look at the satin fabric. "And isn't that a little fancy for Mr. Belding?"

"It's not Mr. Belding's," Lisa said. "It's probably Mrs. Belding's. I had no idea. When I unzipped the bag, I thought I'd just see one of Mr. B.'s drippy suits. I'm really trying to advise him on his wardrobe. But instead I found this!" Lisa reached out to finger the satin. "It's an original Antonio Origami."

"Who?" Screech asked.

"He's the greatest Italian designer *ever*," Lisa said. "All the Hollywood stars wear him. His designs are incredible. I only have two questions: First, what is an original Origami doing hanging in Mr. B.'s closet? I can't tell you how expensive this dress is. Mr. Belding is strictly an outlet kind of guy."

"What's the second question?" Screech asked.

Lisa put her glass down and began to push Screech toward the door. "How soon can you get out of here so I can try it on?"

Screech dug in his rubber heels. "Lisa! You can't! What if something happens?"

"Nothing will happen," Lisa assured him. "I'll just try it on for two seconds and then put it back on the hanger. I promise. What can happen in Mr. Belding's office?"

"I don't know, myself," Screech said as Lisa pushed him through the door. "You'd have to ask Zack. He's in here all the time."

▲   ▼   ▲

Slater pulled Kelly into a grassy spot underneath the bleachers. "Right here is perfect," he said sitting down. "We'll have plenty of privacy."

"Are you sure?" Kelly asked mischievously. "With the way things have gone lately, I wouldn't be surprised if the Bayside marching band came through here right about now."

"I know," Slater agreed with a laugh. "Since we've been back from New Mexico, we've always been in a crowd."

"And we never get a chance to really talk," Kelly agreed.

Slater and Kelly looked at each other. Kelly shifted uncomfortably. Now that they *were* able to talk, she wasn't sure what to say.

"You start," Kelly said.

"Me?" Slater asked nervously.

Kelly nodded.

Slater played with her fingers, then entwined them in his. "Kelly, if you're looking for answers about what we should do, I don't have any," he said. "I really don't want to hurt Jessie. And Zack is my best buddy. But I really care about you."

"I care about you, too," Kelly said softly.

"And I had so much fun with you in Santa Fe," Slater went on. "I mean, I always thought you were gorgeous and nice and funny. You know that. But in Santa Fe, I feel like I got to know the real you. And I really liked her." Slater gazed at Kelly, a sincere look in his soft, dark brown eyes. "I want to get to know her even better."

"I feel the same way, Slater," Kelly said. "But—"

Slater dropped her hand. "I know. That 'but' is going to kill us, every time. Look, Jessie knows where I stand. I'm not happy with her anymore. She's just refusing to see it. Which is typical for Jess. She sees what she wants to see."

"Things with Zack have changed, too," Kelly agreed with a sigh. "I just can't act the way I did before. I'm always thinking about you," she admitted softly.

Slater felt hope wash over him. He'd been wondering if Kelly really felt the same way about him as he did about her. Now he knew she did. That gave him the courage to do something he'd been unsure about.

He'd been carrying around a present that he had bought for Kelly in Santa Fe. He'd been afraid to give it to her when things were so uncertain. What if she'd thought it was too soon for him to give her something? The last thing he wanted to do was scare her away.

Slater reached into his pocket. "I have something for you, Kelly. I picked it out just for you, but I wasn't sure whether to give it to you or not."

"Why not?" Kelly asked.

"Well, because I wasn't sure what was going to happen with us," Slater admitted. "But even if nothing *does* happen between us, I still want you to always remember how I felt."

Slater took a small white box out of his pocket and held it out to Kelly.

Kelly felt touched by Slater's hesitant manner. She'd never realized Slater could be shy. It made her like him even more.

"Gosh, Slater," she said. "I don't know what to say except thank you."

Slater grinned. "You didn't open it yet."

Kelly smiled back. "I don't have to. I know it's going to be perfect."

"Slater!"

Kelly and Slater turned around. Jessie was standing above them, Zack by her side.

"Uh, Jessie!" Slater tried to rise, but he bumped his head against the bleachers. "Yeow," he said, rubbing the top of his head.

"I guess you deserved that," Jessie said.

"I guess I did. Listen, Jessie, if you'd calm down, I'll try to exp—"

"Calm down?" Jessie exclaimed. "How can I calm down when you kept a secret from me?"

"Well—"

"You bought me a present!" Jessie said happily. She dropped to her knees and threw her arms around Slater. "You're the best boyfriend in the world!"

"Uh . . . um . . . gee . . . ," Slater said.

"I'm sorry to spoil the surprise," Jessie said, breaking away from him and taking the box. "Were you going to show it to Kelly to make sure I'd like it? Don't you know I'd love anything you bought for me?"

"W-well, um . . . ," Slater stammered.

Excitedly, Jessie tore open the box. She lifted out a silver pendant and chain. She held it up to the light and watched as it twirled.

"It's beautiful," she breathed.

"It sure is," Kelly murmured. She recognized the necklace right away. She'd admired it in a shop in Santa Fe. Slater had probably noticed her trying it on and then putting it back reluctantly because she couldn't afford it. He was so sweet!

"Oh, Slater. Will you put it on for me?" Jessie asked, turning around so that Slater could fasten the necklace. She faced Kelly. "How does it look?"

"It looks gorgeous, Jessie," Kelly assured her. It *did* look gorgeous.

Jessie turned back to Slater, her eyes moist. "Here you have every reason to hate me, and you go and buy me a present. I just can't believe it.

You're the greatest." She threw her arms around his neck again. Slater looked at Kelly over Jessie's shoulder, his face set grimly.

Zack crouched down. "Jessie, enough with the love fest, okay? I see Mr. Belding heading this way. We'd better split."

Jessie kissed Slater on the cheek. "See you at lunch," she said. "And thank you again for my beautiful present."

As soon as Jessie and Zack were out of earshot, Kelly turned to Slater. "Don't worry, Slater," she said quickly. "I understand. You couldn't tell Jessie the necklace was for me. Not when she was so excited. It's not your fault."

Slater still looked upset. He was staring after Jessie with glazed eyes.

"Really, Slater. I understand," Kelly said, patting his arm. "It's the thought that counts. I'm incredibly touched that you bought me that pendant. That's what means the most."

Slater turned to her. "It's not a pendant," he said woodenly. "It's a locket."

"That's okay," Kelly said soothingly. "I love lockets, but—"

"You don't understand, Kelly," Slater said, stopping her. "The locket opens. And there's an inscription on the inside."

Suddenly Kelly felt very nervous. "There is? What does it say?"

Slater swallowed. "It says '*To K, Let's begin. A.C.*'"

Kelly's hand flew up to her mouth in horror. "So as soon as Jessie figures out it's a locket and opens it—"

"She'll know about us," Slater finished. "Kelly, we have to get that locket back!"

Chapter 3

▲ ▼ ▲ ▼ ▲

Lisa twirled excitedly for Screech as the satin of the dress whirled around her legs. "Isn't it to die for?" she breathed.

"I don't know if it's to *die* for," Screech said nervously as he peeked out into the hall. "But it could be to get *detention* for."

Lisa ran her hands down the seams. "It's perfect," she said. "It's lucky Mrs. B. and I are the same size. How do I look, Screech?"

"Great, Lisa," Screech said, still peering out into the hall.

"You're not even looking!" Lisa protested.

"What if Mr. Belding comes, Lisa?" Screech worried. "He won't even let someone borrow his fountain pen. Can you imagine if he saw you in his wife's dress?"

"He won't. He's too busy patrolling the cleanup." Lisa craned her neck to see herself in the small mirror hanging on Mr. Belding's open closet door. "How's the hemline, Screech? Is it flattering? Do you think it's too long?"

"I don't think it's been that long," Screech said, still peering into the hall. "You've only had it on for about five minutes."

Lisa sighed. Men just didn't get it. They never knew what was *really* important. Hemlines were positively *crucial*.

Lisa had an inspiration. She wheeled over Mr. Belding's desk chair and positioned it in front of the mirror. Using the desk as a boost, she carefully balanced on the chair. Then she looked at the hemline in the mirror.

"It *is* perfect," she said, inspecting the dress with a critical eye. "For Mrs. B. But I think I'd raise the hem about an inch." Lisa hiked up the dress, surveying different lengths for the perfect proportion.

"Lisa, you have to take that dress off!" Screech ordered as he popped back inside.

"Screech!" Jessie exclaimed as she stood in the doorway. "What did you just say?"

"You don't understand, Jessie," Screech told her nervously. "It's a Pastrami!"

"Pastrami? Where? I'm starving," Jessie said.

"Not *Pastrami*, Screech. *Origami*," Lisa corrected.

"You're losing me," Jessie said. "Pastrami on rye I know. But Origami?"

"It's Mrs. Belding's designer dress," Screech explained, pointing at Lisa. "I just know we're going to get caught."

Lisa shot an impish smile at Jessie. "I couldn't resist. Isn't it gorgeous?"

"Wow," Jessie said. "That *is* gorgeous. Is it really an Origami? Do you think Mrs. B. would lend it to me sometime?"

Lisa laughed as she twisted to see herself from behind. "*She* might. But I don't think Mr. Belding would."

"I don't see why not," Jessie protested. "It's not even his size."

She and Lisa giggled. "Listen up, you guys," Jessie said, changing the subject. "I came up here to see if you want to have lunch at the Max. Zack and I are starving."

"Sure," Lisa said. She started to unbutton one of the tiny mother-of-pearl buttons on the sleeve cuff. "Just let me—oh, darn."

"What is it?" Jessie asked.

"The button just popped off," Lisa said.

"Oh, my gosh!" Screech exclaimed, his frizzy curls vibrating with anxiety.

"Now, don't pop your cork, Screech," Lisa said. "It will take me two seconds to sew it back on. I have a sewing kit in my locker."

"I'll find the button for you," Screech offered. He dropped to his knees and began searching the carpet.

Just then Zack sauntered in, eating a hot dog. "I thought I'd have a snack before we ate," he said. "I was starv—"

But Zack didn't get to finish his sentence. He tripped over Screech and went sprawling. The next thing anyone knew, the hot dog had spurted out of his hands and was flying through the air. Jessie vaulted across the desk to try and catch it, but she only succeeded in batting it slightly off course. But Lisa was already leaping off the chair to get out of the way. She connected with the hot dog in midair, and it hit her dead on, right on the front of the dress.

For a moment, everyone was silent. Then Lisa let out a wail.

"Zaaaaack! How could you?"

"How could I? How could Screech?" Zack

protested from the floor. "What was he doing crawling around in front of the doorway?"

Lisa looked down at the bright yellow stain on the dress. She peered closer and saw some flecks of red. "Catsup, too! I can't believe this. Zack, why can't you be a purist when it comes to your dogs? Mustard *and* catsup?"

"You shouldn't be eating hot dogs at all," Jessie scolded him. "They're full of fat and little rat tails, don't you know that?"

Zack stood up. "Hey, get off my case, guys. It wasn't my fault. It was Screech's fault for tripping me. And Jessie's for batting the hot dog right at Lisa. She hit the bull's-eye."

"I might as well admit it. It's my fault for trying on Mrs. Belding's dress in the first place," Lisa finished sadly.

"That's Mrs. Belding's dress?" Zack gulped. "Wow. Then it is *definitely* your fault."

"It's nobody's fault," Jessie sighed. "And everybody's, I guess. It was a stupid accident."

"Hey, no problem," Zack said. "What's the big deal? So we got a little mustard on Mrs. B.'s party dress. We can pay for the dry cleaning. What will it cost, ten bucks?"

Lisa, Jessie, and Screech exchanged a glance.

"Fifteen?" Zack asked, picking up the hot dog

and examining it. He gingerly picked off a carpet hair. Then he shrugged and tossed the dog into the garbage. "What a waste," he said. "Screech, you owe me another one. Screech? You look like you're going to pass out. Okay, okay. I'll buy my own dog. What is *with* you guys?"

"Zack, this dress is an Origami," Lisa said. "It's practically priceless. You can't send it to any old dry cleaner."

"When you say *priceless* you mean Mr. B. didn't pay for it, right?" Zack asked uneasily. "Like it's a hand-me-down, right?"

Lisa shook her head. "I mean it's worth mondo bucks," she said.

"How much is mondo bucks?" Zack asked nervously.

"Somewhere between *yeeeeooooowww!* and *zoooowieeee*," Screech said solemnly.

"Zowie?" Zack gave a low whistle. "That's expensive."

"Shhhh!" Jessie suddenly warned in a whisper. "I hear something."

Screech's skinny face paled. "It's him! It's Mr. Belding!" he hissed.

"Lisa, get that dress off!" Jessie said frantically.

"Screech and I will go out and stall him," Zack said in a low voice. He grabbed Screech by the elbow, and they slithered into the hallway, closing the door behind them.

"Hurry, Lisa," Jessie hissed. She tugged at the zipper while Lisa frantically unbuttoned the cuffs. From outside the door, they heard Zack's voice.

"Hey, Kelly, Slater. Mr. B.! I'm so glad I ran into you. I'm having so much fun today."

"You don't say, Zack," Mr. B. said dryly.

"Here," Lisa whispered, handing Jessie the dress. "The hanger's on the desk."

"Oh, I *do* say," Zack said. "Boy, are we enjoying School Cleanup Day or what, gang? It's the most fun I've had since my trig exam. Just kidding, heh, heh. It just warms my heart to be true to my school. Don't you feel the same way, Kelly?"

"Sure I do," Kelly said. "But since when do you feel that way?"

"Mr. Belding was just about to show us something in his office, Zack," Slater said pointedly.

"Where's the garment bag?" Jessie muttered.

Lisa looked around wildly as she buckled herself back into her corduroy overalls. "I don't know!"

"What's that, Mr. B.?" Zack asked.

"Well, it's a surprise for Mrs. B.," Mr. Belding said proudly. "You see, she recently became a docent at the Modern Art Museum of Los Angeles."

"Wow," Zack said. "That's really impressive."

"Wow," Screech echoed. "It *is*. Um, Mr. Belding, what's a docent?"

"A docent leads tours at a museum or art gallery," Mr. Belding said proudly. "They really have to know a lot about art. A lot of society women are docents. Mrs. Belding was thrilled to be accepted there. She's a big art lover."

"And I bet she's a very decent docent," Screech said, nodding.

"Mr. Belding was telling us that he's going to a big cocktail party at MAMLA tonight," Kelly explained.

"Mamla? Is that a new club?" Zack asked.

"Don't be ridiculous, Zack," Screech said. "We studied *Mamla* in English class. It's a great play by William Shakespeare."

"That's *Hamlet*, Screech," Slater said.

"MAMLA is the acronym for the Modern Art Museum of Los Angeles," Kelly explained.

"And I bought her a very special dress for the occasion," Mr. Belding said. "It practically cost as much as my car."

Meanwhile, inside the office, Lisa had

crawled under the desk and found the garment bag. She threw it at Jessie, who frantically started to stuff the dress into it.

"I'd just love to see it, Mr. B.," Kelly said.

"Well, come on in," Mr. Belding said.

"Wait!" Zack blurted. "I mean, I wanted to ask you something first, Mr. B."

Mr. Belding sounded impatient. "What is it, Zack?"

Jessie and Lisa cracked heads as they scrambled for the closet.

"Um, when separating paper and plastic, where do the milk cartons go?" Zack said. "Because they're plastic-coated paper, you know."

"Read the manual, Zack," Mr. Belding said. "It's posted right on the wall in the cafeteria."

Lisa placed the dress on the hook and closed the closet door.

"Right, but—"

"That's enough, Zack," Mr. Belding said, and opened the door.

Lisa and Jessie stood in front of the closet, smiling innocently.

"What are you girls doing in here?" Mr. Belding asked, frowning.

"Recycling old memos," Lisa said. "Miss

Mazursky had a pile of them, so we figured you did, too."

"No, I don't," Mr. Belding said. "Miss Mazursky files all my memos."

"Show us the dress, Mr. Belding," Kelly prompted. "Ow!" she cried as Zack stepped on her foot.

"I wanted to ask you, Mr. Belding," Zack said. "What do you think the role of the principal is in the nineties?"

"Later, Zack." Mr. Belding put his hand on the closet knob. "Do you kids really want to see the dress?" he asked bashfully. He opened the door an inch.

"*No!*" Lisa, Jessie, Zack, and Screech shouted.

Chapter 4

▲ ▼ ▲ ▼ ▲

Mr. Belding turned around, surprised and a little hurt. "What did you say?"

"They didn't mean it, Mr. B.," Kelly said, shooting the others a puzzled glance. "Of course, we'd love to see your—ow!"

"Was that your foot?" Zack asked innocently.

"It was the last time, too," Kelly muttered, hopping on one foot.

"Personally, I'm dying to see the dress, Mr. B.," Lisa gushed. "We all are, I'm sure. But what we *really* want is . . . is . . . to see you *and* Mrs. B. all dressed up. Together. And seeing the dress now would spoil the surprise."

The frown faded from Mr. Belding's face, and he brightened. "You do? Well, isn't that nice."

"Oh, yes," Lisa elaborated. "It would be just wonderful. To see the two of you, all dressed up, well . . ."

"We live for it," Zack assured him.

"But how are you going to see us?" Mr. Belding asked, frowning again. "Mrs. Belding wouldn't come to my office to get dressed. There's no place to plug in her electric curlers."

"Do you think we could come by your house before you go to the party?" Jessie asked. "We could take pictures."

"Pictures?" Mr. Belding asked happily. "Well, if you insist. . . ."

"Oh, we do," Lisa said firmly. "We absolutely do." She put her hand on Mr. Belding's arm. "Maybe we could even put them up on the bulletin board outside your office. Just to show the rest of Bayside what a sophisticated, handsome principal we really have. I mean, we're so used to seeing you in those terrible drippy suits—"

"They're drip-dry," Mr. Belding sniffed. "I wouldn't call them drippy."

"Oh, I meant drip-dry," Lisa rushed to assure him. "And they're *you*; they positively are. But there's another you, Mr. Belding. Sophisticated. Elegant. Witty. Don't you think your students deserve to see that side of you?"

"Well, when you put it that way, Lisa," Mr. Belding said, straightening his tie, "I really don't see how I can refuse."

"I'm so glad you see the light," Lisa said, firmly closing the closet door.

"So," Mr. Belding said, turning to the rest of the gang. "Here's the schedule. I'm planning to bring the dress home and surprise Mrs. B. around five o'clock. We'll leave for the museum shortly before six, so—"

"We'll be there around five-thirty," Zack said.

"Mr. Belding, you've made us so happy!" Lisa enthused.

"Not to mention relieved," Screech added. "Ow!"

"Well, I'd better check up on the other students," Mr. Belding said, moving toward the door. He stopped and looked down at the carpet. "Whoa. What's this?"

Lisa gasped. She knew what Mr. Belding had seen. It was the button from the dress!

She sprang forward just as Mr. Belding bent over. Lisa slid underneath his reaching fingers and slapped her hand down on the button.

"It's mine!" she cried.

"I wasn't going to steal it, Lisa," Mr. Belding said.

Lisa smiled up at him. "I know," she said. "It's just that I didn't want you to hurt your back."

"It looked kind of familiar, though," Mr. Belding mused. "As a matter of fact, it looked like one of the buttons from—"

"It's my earring," Lisa blurted. "I was wondering where it went."

"I love those earrings," Jessie babbled. "I'm really glad you found it, Lisa."

"Where did you get them?" Mr. Belding asked. "They might be good for Mrs. B. That earring perfectly matches her new dress. Maybe we could hold it up against the dress and—"

"Mr. Belding!" Zack shouted.

"Zack, you don't need to pump up the volume," Mr. Belding said, wincing. "What is it?"

"It's, uh, very important. I have to show you these lima beans," Zack said, taking his arm. "It's a positive disgrace."

"I like lima beans," Mr. Belding said. "What's wrong with them?"

"I can't tell you," Zack said. "I have to *show* you."

Zack led Mr. Belding out of the office. As soon

as the door closed behind him, Lisa slumped back against the desk. "Safe," she said. "For now."

"What is going on?" Kelly asked. "Zack must have broken every toe on my foot."

Lisa quickly explained what happened. By the time she'd taken out the dress again and shown the stain to Slater and Kelly, Zack had returned.

"What did you tell Mr. B. about lima beans?" Jessie asked him curiously.

Zack waved a hand. "I told him there was added salt," he said. "You know how he feels about nutrition. Have we figured out a way to get that stain out yet?"

"Maybe we should try club soda," Kelly suggested. "That's what my mom uses sometimes."

"I say we take it to Tony's While-U-Wait Dry Cleaners," Slater said.

"Wait a second," Zack said. "I'm trying to remember the name of that stain remover my mom used that time I changed my bike chain on the living room rug—"

"You *what*?" Lisa said, wrinkling her nose.

"Hey, it was raining out," Zack said. "You didn't expect me to do it in the driveway, did you? Now, what was it . . . Stain No More? No. Hate That Stain? No . . . "

Slater sidled up to Jessie and pulled her into

the corner of Mr. Belding's office. She smiled at him and fingered her pendant. "Hi," she said softly.

"Hi," Slater said. "Listen, Jess, I was just noticing that chain. I think it's too short for you, don't you?"

"Not at all—"

"No, no, it is, I can tell. Why don't I take the pendant back and get a new chain?" Slater insisted. "You'd have it back tomorrow, no problem."

"Slater, no," Jessie said, closing her fingers around the pendant. "I love the chain. It's sweet of you, but no. It's the perfect length."

"Oh," Slater said. He peered at the pendant. "You know what, though, Jessie? The silver looks tarnished. Yeah, definitely. Why don't you let me take it and polish it up for you. . . . " He reached over to try to undo the clasp.

Jessie wriggled away, laughing. "Don't worry, Slater. I love the pendant. It's perfect. And it's not tarnished at all." She held it up to catch the light. "You see how shiny it is? No way is this coming off my neck."

"*Your* neck?" Lisa asked frantically, overhearing Jessie's last words. "What about *my* neck? We have to save it! Mr. B. is going to kill me! You guys, we just have to come up with a plan."

Screech held up a hand. "Fear not, fair lady. I've come up with a foolproof plan."

"You did, Screech?" Lisa asked dubiously.

"O ye of little faith," Screech intoned.

"Screech, speak English," Lisa pleaded. "You know, the kind we speak in this century. What's your plan?"

"Super Dooper Disappearing Drops," Screech said. "Guaranteed to lift any stain, anytime."

"How can you be sure?" Jessie asked.

"Because I invented it," Screech responded. "It was my last chemistry experiment. It lifted the grease stain right off Mr. Trapezi's tie. You should have seen him! He practically kissed me."

"Where is it, Screech?" Lisa asked. "Can you get it?"

"No problem," Screech said. "I'll just pop up to the lab and rustle up a batch right now. In about twenty minutes, Lisa, all your problems will be solved!"

▲   ▼   ▲

A half hour later, Zack stared at Mrs. Belding's dress. He reached out and touched it with an unsteady finger. "Wow," he said.

Lisa clapped her hands over her eyes. "I can't look anymore."

"Did you say that Mr. Trapezi almost *kissed* you or almost *killed* you?" Slater asked Screech.

"I'd like to kill you," Lisa said. Her voice came out muffled as she peeked between her fingers, then clapped her hands over her eyes again.

The yellow stain on Mrs. Belding's dress was even worse than before. It had grown to be a putrid greenish blob.

"I think it's moving," Kelly whispered, horrified.

"Screech, what went wrong?" Zack asked.

Screech studied a piece of paper. "Maybe it wasn't potassium. Maybe it was magnesium," he mused. "I thought I'd remember the formula. But I guess I didn't." Screech sighed. "I'm really sorry, Lisa. I tried, but I messed up, as usual."

Lisa dropped her hands. Screech looked truly sorry. She didn't want to make him feel worse. "It's okay," she said, patting his arm. "I know you tried, Screech."

"Maybe we should try Tony's While-U-Wait Dry Cleaners after all," Slater said.

Lisa looked at the dress. "What I need isn't a dry cleaner," she said. "I need a whole new dress."

Everyone nodded sadly.

"A whole new dress," Lisa repeated slowly. "That's what we have to do! We have to get a whole new dress!"

"And how are we going to do that, Lisa?" Zack asked. "Does anyone have a few thousand dollars lying around in a bank account somewhere?"

"Or at least a lottery ticket?" Kelly asked with a shrug.

"Listen up, you guys," Lisa said excitedly. "Origami has a showroom in L.A. Why don't we just replace the dress?"

"I repeat, Lisa," Zack said. "With what? Our good looks? That should get us maybe a zipper."

"Speak for yourself, preppy," Slater said with a smirk. "In my case, two sleeves *and* a zipper."

"Maybe we don't need money," Lisa said, thinking hard. "Origami is known for his charitable contributions. He's really a soft touch. What if we can get him to *donate* a dress? We'll appeal to his humanitarian instincts."

"What are you saying, Lisa?" Jessie asked doubtfully. "That we ask him to donate a dress to a good cause?"

"Exactly," Lisa said. "We just won't say what the good cause is."

The gang exchanged glances.

"What else are we going to do?" Lisa pointed out. "In only a few hours, Mr. Belding is going to be bringing home a dress to Mrs. B. And if he brings her this rag, our names are mud."

"Maybe Lisa's right," Zack said. "What do we have to lose?"

"It sounds like a long shot to me," Slater said.

"But it sure beats recycling cans for the school which we'll soon be suspended from if we don't," Jessie said.

"And it beats standing around," Kelly said. "We might as well take a chance."

"Bingo," Zack said. "After all, you can't make an omelette without breaking a few eggs."

"You can't start a fire without chopping some wood," Jessie chimed in.

"You can't go fishing without opening a can of worms," Slater put in.

"And you can't go away for the weekend without leaving a big dish of water for your hamster," Screech finished.

"Screech, how do you do it?" Lisa sighed. "You can always make a weird situation weirder."

"It *is* a special talent," Screech said modestly.

▲   ▼   ▲

Kelly hung back as the gang rushed out of Mr. Belding's office. She tugged on Slater's T-shirt.

"Did you get the necklace?" she whispered.

Slater shook his head. "She won't take it off," he answered in a low voice.

Kelly bit her lip worriedly. "What are we going to do, Slater? She's going to figure out that it's a locket sooner or later."

"I know," Slater agreed. "We're in for some major fireworks. I'm really sorry I got you into this, Kelly."

"It's not your fault," Kelly said, her blue eyes warming as she looked at Slater's worried face. "How could you have known that Jessie would walk up right then?"

"But I *should* have known," Slater said. "Ever since we got back from Santa Fe, Jessie has been sticking to me like glue."

"I understand," Kelly said. "Every time I turn around, Zack is there, too. I guess he feels bad about what's happening between us. Or what's *not* happening. Either way, it makes me feel awful."

"Jessie wants me to fall back in love with her," Slater said. "But all this attention is driving me crazy. It just doesn't feel real. Jessie never followed me around and flattered me like this before. She's turned into this weird pod person."

"She's afraid of losing you," Kelly said.

"The sad part for her is that she already has," Slater said.

Just then Jessie popped her head back into Mr. Belding's office. "There you are," she said to Slater. "Come on, guys. We're all going to drive up to L.A. in Zack's car."

Jessie's necklace swung back and forth. Kelly and Slater stared at it, mesmerized.

"I'll meet you in the parking lot," Jessie said. "But first Lisa and I are going to get her kit and sew that button back on." Her head disappeared, and they listened to her footsteps hurrying away.

"Slater, we have to get that necklace," Kelly said.

"I know," he answered grimly. "Do you think Screech's Super Dooper Disappearing Drops could make an inscription disappear?"

Kelly sighed. "If Jessie finds out, do you think it could make *me* disappear?"

Chapter 5

▲ ▼ ▲ ▼ ▲

The Origami showroom was located in a trendy Los Angeles neighborhood of renovated warehouses. The gang found it easily. They even found a parking spot. What they couldn't come up with was an excuse to go in.

"Origami doesn't see customers here," Lisa fretted. "They go to his store on Rodeo Drive. But this is where Origami works every day. We have to come up with a reason to get in."

The gang regarded the smooth façade of the industrial building. From across the street, it looked like a fortress.

"Maybe we could pretend to be buyers for a department store," Kelly suggested.

"A designer usually knows all the buyers by face, if not by name," Lisa said.

"Why don't Zack and I pretend to be electricians or something?" Slater tried.

"Wait, you guys," Jessie said. "Look. Some people are going in."

The gang watched as a trio of smartly dressed women headed for the front door. Lisa peered at a blond-haired woman in sunglasses.

"That looks like Polly Trebella, the editor of *Mode* magazine," she said. "Maybe there's something going on."

Just as Lisa finished talking, a limousine pulled up and a couple got out. They swept up to the door and also entered the building.

"Something is definitely going on," Zack agreed.

As they stared at the building, a van pulled up in front of them, blocking their view. Out spilled a camera crew. They began unpacking equipment right in front of the gang.

Lisa hailed one of the cameramen. "Hi," she called. "Is that the Origami showroom across the street?"

He nodded in a friendly way. "You here for the resort collection showing?"

"No, we're trying to sneak in," Screech said.

Zack laughed heartily. "That's my assistant," he said. "What a cutup. Of course we're here for the showing. We're journalists."

"Well, you'd better hustle if you want a good spot," the cameraman said with a grimace. "You know how crowded Origami's shows always are."

"Absolutely," Lisa said. "The only thing is, we forgot our press passes." She walked a few steps closer and gave him her prettiest smile. "Can you tell I'm new at this?"

The cameraman grinned back. "We all have to start somewhere."

"I work for this real small paper out of Palisades, and I'm finally getting my first break," Lisa said. "I have a shot at the cover in the Sunday magazine. I really wanted to prove myself to my editor."

"Listen, don't sweat it," he said. "Our second van called in. They broke down on the freeway, and they're not going to make it. There's a pile of press passes on the front seat. Just take what you need."

"Gosh, thank you," Lisa said. "That's really nice of you."

"Always glad to help out a greenhorn. Gotta run, though."

"Wasn't he nice?" Lisa said, turning back to the gang.

"He sure was. Until he said you had green horns!" Screech sputtered. "Why, I oughtta—"

"Down, boy," Kelly said. "He meant Lisa was a tenderfoot."

"I know Lisa has tender feet," Screech said, blushing. "She's very delicate. But that's an awfully personal thing to—"

"Screech, exit this file right now," Lisa ordered. "We have to get moving." She reached into the van and took six press passes.

Kelly looked down at her shorts and T-shirt. "We don't look very much like fashion journalists."

Lisa bit her lip. "You're right. We don't."

"We don't look stylish," Jessie said. "We look like we're ready to clean out the garage."

"Hold on," Zack said. He ran to his car and opened the trunk. He began tossing out bandannas, sweatshirts, a baseball cap, and a camera.

Zack put the baseball cap on backwards. Then he slung the camera around his neck. Lisa showed Slater how to tie a bandanna around his head the way Armando Rex, the world-renowned male model, had made famous. Jessie put on a pair of sunglasses and fluffed out her long curly hair. Kelly tied a scarf around her waist like a sarong. Lisa grabbed a notebook and a pencil.

"That's better," Lisa said in satisfaction. "Let's go crash this party!"

▲   ▼   ▲

"Okay, gang," Zack murmured as they headed across the street. "Just follow me. Remember, the key to getting into any party is *don't hesitate*. Act like you belong."

At the door, a pretty brunette with a distracted air was checking people's credentials against a list. A backlog of people soon collected ahead of Zack and the gang.

"There's a list!" Jessie moaned, panicked.

"And our names are definitely not on it," Slater said.

"Don't worry," Zack said with more confidence than he felt.

Ahead of them, a woman in a fur coat was complaining loudly. "I do not *believe* this," she said. "If Antonio wasn't such a *genius*, I'd turn around and go right home. This is totally unacceptable."

"Maybe it wouldn't be so bad if you weren't wearing dead animal skins on a seventy-degree day," Jessie muttered.

Lisa poked her. "Don't start," she warned. "We can't call attention to ourselves, remember?"

A tall, gaunt woman dressed in a tailored black suit appeared at the brunette's shoulder. "What's the problem, Marianne?" she asked. Her voice dripped icicles.

"Oh, nothing, Miss Quirk. You said to check every name against the list, and it takes, uh, well, time—"

"Did you alphabetize the list?" Miss Quirk snapped.

The pretty young woman turned pale. "No," she practically whispered. "No one told me to."

"Does someone have to tell you to get up in the morning, or can you figure that one out by yourself?" Miss Quirk hissed.

"Whew," Kelly murmured underneath her breath. "That woman is scary."

"I'm terrified," Lisa said with a shiver.

"I wouldn't want to meet her in a dark alley," Slater said. "She'd probably drain my blood."

Miss Quirk extended a bony white hand to the woman in the fur coat. "Adelaide, darling, please come this way. Antonio made me save a very special seat for you in the first row."

Miss Quirk gave Marianne a daggerlike look as she escorted Madame Fur past her.

"Are you sure we can get in?" Lisa whispered to Zack.

"Now I'm *positive* we can," Zack answered.

When they reached Marianne, Zack fired out their names in a bored tone. "From the Palisades *Gazette*," he said. "We did a feature on Antonio last year."

"Yes, of course," Marianne said, hurriedly running her finger down the list. "But I don't see your names here. Or your paper."

"What?" Zack asked in an incredulous tone. "This is totally unacceptable."

"Let me check again," Marianne said. Behind Zack, a group of women began to grumble. Marianne looked uneasily back into the Origami showroom.

Zack put his hand over Marianne's. "Don't bother checking. Obviously someone messed up, and I do hope it wasn't you. We'll just wait for Miss Quirk."

Marianne gulped. "Wait? For Miss Quirk?"

"She and I go way back," Zack assured her. "Does she have dinner plans, do you know?"

"D-dinner plans?" Marianne stammered.

"We're like this," Zack said, holding up two fingers pressed together. "She's a doll, don't you think?"

"There she is now," Jessie said. She wiggled her fingers at the empty space beyond Marianne's shoulder.

"Youcangoaheadin," Marianne said quickly.

"Thank you, darling," Zack said, sweeping past her.

Lisa giggled as they entered the gray-carpeted hallway. "Just be glad we didn't see Miss Quirk," she said. "I sure wouldn't want to have to tangle with her."

With people pushing behind them and ahead of them, they made their way down a long corridor. To the right, gigantic double doors in brushed steel were thrown open. They could see a long room crowded with gray velvet chairs that were rapidly filling up with people. A long runway ran from a stage at the front.

Zack turned and saw a door at the end of the corridor. "Let's try this way," he whispered.

When he opened the door, he found a stairway leading upward. "The offices are probably upstairs," he guessed. "Come on."

He pulled Lisa, who pulled Jessie, who pulled Screech, who pulled Slater, who pulled Kelly into the stairwell. They hurried up the stairs to the second floor. Zack slowly pushed open the door at the top of the stairs.

The door opened into a huge workroom. Swatches of material were pinned up next to sketches on a board that ran almost the entire length of the room. Dressmaker's dummies stood around as if they were guarding the space. And along the opposite wall were racks and racks of gorgeous dresses in every color and fabric imaginable.

"Have I died and gone to heaven?" Lisa breathed. She walked slowly toward the dresses and ran her hands along the rustling silks and satins.

"We have to get busy," Zack said. "The first step is to find Mrs. Belding's dress."

"Then we can bring it to Mr. Origami and ask if he'll donate it to charity, right?" Jessie said.

"This long shot is so long that I need a telescope to see it," Slater said, groaning.

"Hold it," Zack said. "Maybe there's an easier way. What if we *don't* talk to Origami and smuggle the dress out of the building? We can take it back to Palisades and bring Mrs. Belding's dress back here. We can pull the old switcheroo. Origami will probably think one of the models stained the sample."

"It might be hard to smuggle the dress out of the building," Slater said. "I'm sure their security is pretty tight."

"We got in, didn't we?"

"But I saw them checking bags," Lisa said worriedly. "Besides, that plan sounds kind of like stealing to me."

"Me, too," Kelly agreed. "It would be wrong."

"Not to mention the trouble we'd be in if we did get caught," Zack said with a sigh.

"Back to Plan A," Lisa said. "We might as well make sure there even is a dress. We can think of how to approach Mr. Origami after we find it."

Everyone split up and began going through the racks. Lisa lingered over each gorgeous outfit. Sigh after sigh drifted from her mouth.

"Lisa," Slater called after a few minutes, "you're supposed to be trying to find Mrs. Belding's dress. Not a dress for the prom."

"I know," Lisa said as she reluctantly replaced a pink satin dress on the rack. "But I can't help it. I feel like a kid in a candy store."

"Look at this one," Kelly said, slipping out an ice blue silk sheath. "Isn't it pretty?"

"That would look incredible on you, momma," Slater said appreciatively. "It would really bring out those beautiful eyes of yours."

"Hey, watch it," Zack said jovially. "Those are my girlfriend's eyes you're talking about."

Jessie giggled. "Since when are you so fashion conscious, Slater?"

"Uh, I guess the place is rubbing off on me," Slater mumbled.

Blushing, Kelly hurriedly replaced the dress in the rack. "I don't see Mrs. Belding's dress," she said, quickly flipping through several summer suits.

"I found it!" Lisa crowed. She drew out a lilac satin dress.

"Lisa, Mrs. Belding's dress is blue," Jessie pointed out.

"I *know*," Lisa said. "Do you think Mr. Belding is color-blind?"

"That is a pretty color," Kelly said. "Maybe he won't remember."

"He'll remember," Zack said. "Remember when I dinged the side of his Miata in the parking lot and Slater repainted it for me? Mr. B. spotted the job from fifty paces. He kept saying that his paint was scarlet and Slater had touched it up with crimson."

"Oh, well," Lisa said, still holding up the dress. "If you're sure that—"

"May I ask what you people are doing here?"

The voice sounded like a whip cracking over their heads. It sounded like a pointed dagger whistling through the air.

Their hearts sank right into their shoes. They knew who it belonged to.

Miss Quirk stood at the entrance to the workroom. Zack was positive that fire whooshed from her skinny nostrils as she took a few steps forward into the room.

"I repeat," she said. "What are you doing here?"

For the first time in his life, Zack couldn't think of a thing to say. His tongue seemed frozen to the roof of his mouth. He'd faced down furious teachers, exasperated coaches, even beefy security guards.

But this woman was *serious* trouble.

He was positive there was a skeleton of steel underneath that tailored black suit. From behind the bright red line that passed as a mouth, he knew razor-sharp teeth lurked.

"We just—," Lisa started.

"We were—," Slater said.

"Uh—," Jessie said.

Miss Quirk turned on a spiked black heel and reached for a white telephone. "How eloquent you are. I'm happy to see you all live up to your appearances. But don't tax yourself with an attempt at speech. Because I'm calling the police!"

Chapter 6

▲ ▼ ▲ ▼ ▲

Zack strode forward and put his hand on the phone. "Please," he said. "No more headlines. They give Fifi migraines, and then she has to stay in bed for days."

"Who, may I ask, is Fifi?" Miss Quirk sniffed. "Your poodle?"

Zack quickly went back to Kelly and pushed her forward a few steps. "Don't you recognize the famous French supermodel Fifi La Peu?"

"Who?" Miss Quirk asked.

Zack poked Kelly in the back. She felt herself start to tremble. But she told herself sternly to pull herself together. She wanted to be an actress, didn't she? Well, here was the role of a lifetime.

"Am I wrong to be 'ere?" she asked plaintively in a heavy French accent. "I was looking for my leetle outfit for ze show. No one told me where to go for eet."

"That Marianne again," Miss Quirk muttered. "She's impossible!"

"Oh, no, Mees Marianne was *charmante*," Kelly said quickly. She didn't want to get that nice woman fired. "She ees a leetle cabbage, that one. But everyzing else—poof! Ees outrageous downstairs! Zo disorganized! I weel have to talk to my cher Antonio about zees!"

Zack looked at Kelly, stunned. His quiet, sweet girlfriend was having a real French snit. He stifled a guffaw and turned it into a cough.

"And who is that?" Miss Quirk said, pointing to Zack.

"Zees? Zees is my 'airdresser," Kelly said. She ruffled Zack's hair. "I nev-air travel without heem." She pointed to Lisa. "And zees ees my makeup artiste—ze wizard with ze mascara wand. And zees," she said, indicating Jessie, "ees my publiceest. Zees is my pair-son-al trainer," she said, feeling Slater's muscle and giving an appreciative "Ooooo."

"And zees—" Kelly stopped when she got to Screech. She thought frantically, but her mind was a blank. "And zees ees—ees my—"

"Dentist!" Screech suggested helpfully.

"Denteest. Exactly," Kelly said. She shrugged at Miss Quirk. "My teeth need ze polish, no? 'Ow about you? Would you like to borrow heem?"

Miss Quirk looked confused. "I don't think so. I go to my cousin Ralph."

"*Bon, bon.* Ooooo—zat ees my favorite candy. Ze bonbons. Perhaps you left some in my dressing room, no?" Kelly gave a trill of a laugh. "But Antonio weel scold me eef I am late. I must be leetle bird and fly away! Au revoir!"

Tossing her long dark hair over her shoulder and blowing Miss Quirk a kiss, Kelly headed for the door. The gang followed on her heels as fast as they could.

As soon as they reached the safety of the first floor, they burst out laughing.

"You were awesome," Slater told Kelly.

"That's my girl," Zack said, slinging an arm around her shoulders. Slater looked away.

"I was so scared!" Kelly admitted, laughing.

"You see, Kelly?" Zack said. "I always said you had a talent for scamming. There's only one thing, though. Did you have to make me your 'air-dresser?"

Everybody laughed at Zack's comical expression.

"We'd better lie low," Jessie advised. "If Miss Quirk figures out that Kelly isn't in the fashion show, she'll come looking for us."

"But we can't leave yet!" Lisa cried.

"We're not leaving," Slater assured her. "We'd better hurry, though. We don't want to miss the fashion show." He clapped a hand to his forehead. "I can't believe what I just said."

"I can't, either," Jessie said, laughing. "Maybe you 'ave a taste for zis business, *Monsieur* Slater."

The gang hurried down the corridor and slipped into the main showroom. The long room was jammed with people, but Slater found them places in the back along a curtained wall. "This way, if Miss Quirk walks by, we can duck behind the curtain," he said in a low tone as they took their places.

Kelly found herself standing between Zack and Slater. She felt Slater's hand creep into hers and give it a squeeze. She turned slightly to shield him from Zack, but she stepped on Zack's foot.

"Oops, sorry," she told Zack.

"For what?" he said, his eyes on the stage as the show began.

Meanwhile, on the other side of Slater, Jessie decided to take advantage of the crowd by nestling closer to his side. But she ended up jabbing him with her elbow.

"Sorry, Slater," she whispered.

"What did you do now?" he asked.

"Screech, you're pulling my hair!" Lisa said, tugging on her ponytail.

"No, I'm not," Screech said.

"Are you saying I'm imagining it?"

"No. But you did just step on my foot. Not that I minded, oh, lovely one—"

Suddenly a pronounced whisper came from behind the curtain. "Will you all please shut up? I'm trying to work!"

The gang exchanged glances.

"We didn't imagine *that*," Lisa said.

They pulled aside the curtain. A tall, slim guy dressed in a black turtleneck and jeans blinked at them behind wire-rimmed glasses.

"Can I help you?" he said.

"What are you doing?" Zack asked. "Do you get your kicks out of hiding behind curtains and trying to scare people?"

"I wasn't trying to scare you," the guy said. "I was trying to see the show."

Lisa peeked over his shoulder. "He's sketching."

"Who are you?" Kelly asked. "One of Origami's assistants?"

"Hardly," the guy said. He ran his hand through his tousled brown hair, making it even messier. "I'm much more talented than those hacks. My name is Willy Kozinski. I'm a fashion designer."

Lisa gasped. "I know what you're doing! You're stealing Origami's designs!"

"I'm not stealing," Willy Kozinski said haughtily. "I'm *borrowing*."

"It happens all the time," Lisa said. She turned to the guys. "Smaller fashion companies copy the outfits of famous designers, only they produce them for the mass market. They use cheaper materials and skimp on the detailing."

Willy winced at the description. "*I* don't skimp," he insisted. "And I only steal from the best. Sometimes I even do it better. Now, I don't want to be rude, but if the dragon lady sees me, I'm out on my ear, so—"

"I think we know who you're talking about," Kelly said. "Miss Quirk, right?"

Willy shuddered. "That woman should be in a cage."

"You said it," Zack agreed.

"She nearly threw us out," Jessie said.

"Listen, guys, can you do me a favor?" Willy

asked. "If you'd just gather around me, you could act as a shield. I could do my sketches. It's getting awfully hot behind this curtain."

"Of course," Kelly said.

"Thanks for helping me out," Willy said gratefully. "Origami is my favorite designer, and the faster I can rip him off, the more money I'll make. Stealing is the sincerest form of flattery, you know," he said, his pencil flying over the paper as he sketched a summer suit.

"We're happy to help," Lisa said, positioning herself in front of Willy.

"Sure, Willy," Zack said. An idea had formed in his head, and as usual, it was brilliant. An added bonus was that it might even work!

He turned back to their new friend. "And after the show, maybe you can do a little something to help *us* out."

▲   ▼   ▲

The fashion show ended with Origami's resort collection wedding dress: a pair of tiny shorts made out of white silk with a train of pink roses sewn on fluttering gauze. The crowd erupted in applause. A figure in black left the wings of the stage and moved toward the audience.

"Uh-oh. Quirk alert," Willy murmured, stuffing his sketch pad in his knapsack.

Miss Quirk moved quickly through the crowd, heading for the back of the room.

Lisa looked around wildly. "We'll never get out of here in time!" she exclaimed. "It's too crowded."

"No sweat," Willy said. "Follow me, gang."

Instead of leaving through the double doors, Willy went toward the stage. There was a door hidden behind the curtains along the wall.

"This is how the models slip in and out so they don't have to deal with the crowds," Willy explained, pushing open the door.

They found themselves in a short alley that ran along the side of the building. Willy led them down the alley, and they ended up on a side street.

"That was the best ever," Willy said, slipping his pad out and flipping through the pages. "Usually Quirk spots me about halfway through the show. But today I think I got a sketch of every single outfit. Hot dog!"

Lisa winced. "Please, don't remind us."

Willy gave her a quizzical grin. "So what can I do for you guys?"

Zack quickly outlined the problem. Then Lisa described the dress. Even before she'd gotten to the underskirt of pale pink, Willy nodded.

"I knocked that dress off for my last collection," he said.

Screech slumped in disappointment. "So you don't have it?"

"No, Screech," Lisa said. *"Knocked off* means he copied it."

"I even did it in the same colors," Willy said. "Midnight blue satin with that pale peony underskirt peeking through. It's the work of a genius."

"Origami is my favorite designer, too," Lisa agreed.

"No, I meant me," Willy said. "Only a genius could have made that dress as perfect as Origami did for half the price."

"Half the price?" Lisa asked. "That will still be too much money," she said to the gang.

"Low on cash, huh?" Willy said. "I can relate." He looked at the girls. "Listen, I think I can come up with a way to get you what you want. If you can do me another favor."

"We can try," Kelly said.

"I don't just do knockoffs, you know," Willy said. "I have my own designs. And I've finally raised the money to get them produced. I want to show them to the press, but I can't afford models. So I was thinking. If you girls would agree to model in my show in a couple of weeks, I'd give you the dress for free. Do you think that would be okay?"

Kelly, Jessie, and Lisa looked at each other. Model designer clothes in a fashion show? Willy had to be kidding. They'd do it for nothing.

"That sounds fair," Lisa said.

"More than fair," Kelly agreed.

"We'd be glad to," Jessie said.

Willy grinned at them. "So do we have a deal?"

"It's a deal," the gang said together.

Chapter 7

▲ ▼ ▲ ▼ ▲

Willy's studio was only a few blocks away. It was in a shabby-looking warehouse off a tiny alley.

"Not as posh as Origami's place, but give me a few years," he said cheerfully as he wrestled with the lock.

They climbed up a gloomy wooden staircase until they were at the top. Willy opened the lock to another door and they walked into a loft space that was bright and airy. Windows ran along one whole wall and two skylights let in plenty of light. Along the back wall was a balcony where rolls of fabric were kept.

The workroom itself didn't look much different from Origami's. It was filled with long tables piled with sketch pads and dressmaker's dummies and sewing machines.

"The actual work is done in a factory," Willy explained as he tossed his knapsack onto a cluttered desk. "But we do all the mock-ups here. My backer is a big company called Acrilon Industries. They own a bunch of different fashion companies. You might have heard of their sportswear line, Surf City. This is their dressy line, called Eleganza."

"I have some clothes from Surf City," Lisa said. "And I've looked at dresses from Eleganza, but I haven't been able to afford them."

"I'll put you girls on the list for our sample sales if you want," Willy said. "Then you can buy dresses below wholesale."

"I like the sound of that," Jessie said.

"Me, too," Kelly said. "I'd love to be able to afford a really beautiful dress."

"Let me get out the dress you want so you can take a look," Willy said. "I have the whole line here."

Willy disappeared into a back room and returned a few seconds later with a dark blue dress.

"That's it!" Jessie cried.

"We're saved," Zack said fervently.

"It looks like a perfect match," Kelly said.

Lisa took it from Willy and frowned. "Hold on," she said. "I can tell with one look that this isn't an Origami."

"What are you talking about?" Willy bristled. "It's an exact copy. I even got a special deal on the silk, so I was able to match Origami's fabric almost exactly. As a matter of fact, I think this dress is even better than Origami's."

"How so?" Zack asked, interested.

Willy grinned. "It's cheaper."

"I'm sorry, Willy," Lisa said. "It's a nice dress. But it just isn't an Origami. And if *I* can tell it's a knockoff, you can bet other people will be able to."

"But will Mr. Belding?" Slater wondered.

"Or even Mrs. Belding?" Zack pointed out. "It's not like she wears designer clothes all the time."

"It doesn't matter, Zack," Lisa said, turning to him. "Because she'll be with people who do. What if this new crowd she's hanging around with can tell? We can't embarrass Mrs. B. that way! You know how snobby those people are."

The gang stopped, sunk in gloom. Lisa was right. They really liked Mrs. Belding, and they wanted her to succeed at the museum. Would the society crowd there take her seriously in a dress they knew was a knockoff?

"And what if Mrs. B. wants to exchange it or get it altered someday?" Jessie pointed out. "She's bound to find out it's not the real thing sometime."

Suddenly Zack snapped his fingers. "I've got it, gang," he said. "It doesn't matter if this dress will fool anyone or not. Because I just came up with the second part of the plan. We have to get back to Palisades! We still have to switch this dress with the Origami. I'll tell you the rest of my plan on the way."

"Whoa, hold on, guys," Willy said. "Before you go, the girls have to try on one of my dresses. I have to get their sizes for my show."

Zack looked at his watch. "We have a little time. No sweat."

"No sweat is right," Willy said, taking a silk dress off the rack. "Don't perspire in my dresses, girls. Follow me to the fitting rooms."

He motioned to them to come behind a divider, into the back room of the loft. There, he chose the dresses he wanted them to try.

Kelly turned out to be a perfect fit for Willy's sample size. But Jessie was a little too tall, and Lisa was a little too short.

"Just hang on a minute," Willy said. He looped a tape measure around his neck and stuck a pencil behind his ear. "Jessie and Lisa, can you try on a few more dresses?"

"Sure," Lisa said. "We have time. And this is fun."

"Cool," Willy said. "Jessie, how about trying on that green print? I just need to check the hem."

Slater came up behind Jessie. "Maybe I should hold the pendant for you," he said. "I wouldn't want you to lose it."

"I'll be super careful," Jessie promised.

"No, really, Jessie," Slater insisted. He reached up and fumbled with the clasp. "I'd rather keep it in my pocket." He slipped the necklace off her neck.

"I'll be right back," Jessie promised. She walked off toward the fitting rooms, the frothy green dress trailing behind her.

Finally! Slater thought in relief as he fingered the necklace in his pocket. At last he had the locket. Now he just had to find a way to keep it.

▲   ▼   ▲

While Jessie and Lisa tried on a few more dresses, Zack and Screech wandered off to explore the rest of the loft. That gave Slater the perfect opportunity to take Kelly aside.

"Follow me," he whispered, grabbing her hand.

"Slater, where—"

"Shhh," he said, putting a finger to his lips.

Kelly followed him as he tiptoed past the divider into the back space of the loft. She could hear Lisa and Jessie giggling behind a fitting room door. Somewhere farther on, hangers clanged against a rack as Willy swiftly searched for more dresses.

Slater glided past Jessie's and Lisa's voices and came to the last fitting room. He pulled Kelly inside and shut the door.

"Slater, what are you doing?" Kelly whispered. "They'll catch us."

"I don't care," Slater murmured. "I had to be alone with you, Kelly."

Kelly softened. "I know what you mean."

"Kelly, I can't go on like this," Slater said. "I really want to be with you. It's so hard seeing Zack putting his arm around you."

"And it's hard seeing you with Jessie," Kelly said.

"Especially when I want to be with *you*," Slater added.

"Maybe after all this is over, we can talk to Zack and Jessie," Kelly said. "But even if we break up with them, we can't start dating, Slater."

Slater nodded. "We can't," he agreed distractedly, staring at Kelly's wide blue eyes. "Hey, wait a second. We can't?"

"No way," Kelly said. "Think about it, Slater. You can't break up with Jessie on Sunday and then ask me out on Monday! Just think of how much it would hurt her."

"I guess you're right," Slater admitted. "I wasn't thinking. This isn't going to be easy, is it?"

"No, it's not," Kelly said. "Maybe we . . . "

"Don't say it, Kelly," Slater interrupted. "Don't say we shouldn't try."

"But I don't want to hurt anybody," Kelly said.

"I don't, either," Slater said. "But, Kelly, we have to be honest. We have to follow our feelings. Even if something hadn't started between us, you'd still be upset about things with Zack, wouldn't you?"

Kelly nodded. "That trip to Santa Fe was a real eye-opener," she said. "I really saw that as much as I love Zack, he's just not the kind of boyfriend who can make me happy. I've been wanting to talk to him ever since, but we haven't had two seconds alone."

"And I realized the same thing about Jessie and me," Slater said. "Sometimes caring about someone just isn't enough, Kelly. That's what makes this so hard."

"So what do you think we should do?" Kelly asked.

"I think we should follow our hearts," Slater said. "But I think we should be quiet about it for a while. After we have our talks with Zack and Jessie, we can see each other. But we should wait before we make it public."

"I agree," Kelly said. "I hope we can keep it secret." Suddenly she gasped. "Slater, what about the locket?"

"That's what I wanted to tell you. I got it back from Jessie," Slater said. "I told her I didn't want it to get lost while she was trying on outfits."

"But you're going to have to give it back to her, aren't you?"

"Not if *I* lose it," Slater said.

"How are you going to explain that?" Kelly asked doubtfully. "You took it for safekeeping."

Slater reached into his pocket and turned it inside out for Kelly. There was a big hole in the bottom. "I used one of Willy's seam rippers to make a hole in my pocket," he said. "And I left the locket lying on the floor near a bunch of old fabric swatches. We'll be in too much of a hurry to search for it today, but I'll come back next week and find it. Then I can get the inscription changed and give it back to Jessie."

"Slater, that's brilliant!" Kelly said. "That way Jessie won't get hurt."

"You see?" Slater murmured, slipping his arms around her. "Zack's not the only one who can pull a scam. And you were pretty good in that department, too, Mademoiselle Fifi," he teased.

"You zink I 'ave ze right stuff, zen?" Kelly asked impishly.

"Whoa, momma," Slater said, pulling Kelly closer. "You *definitely* have ze right stuff."

He leaned down and brushed his lips against hers. "Now, *zat* is ze right stuff," Kelly murmured.

"Shall we try again?" Slater asked, dipping his head down toward Kelly's uplifted face.

"Kelly!"

It was Jessie's voice, and it was right outside their door. Slater froze. Kelly looked at him, wide-eyed.

"Kel-ly! We're ready to head out!"

Footsteps approached Jessie. "Have you seen her?" Zack asked.

"No," Jessie said. "I can't imagine where she went."

"Well, we have to look for Slater, too," Zack said. "We have to hustle or we'll be late getting the dress back before Mr. Belding finds out."

"I'll look upstairs," Jessie said.

"I'll try the hall," Zack said.

Kelly felt her heartbeat slow down as the footsteps receded. "We'd better get out of here," she whispered.

They tiptoed to the door and peeked out. No one was in sight. Kelly slipped out first. She hurried to the front part of the loft, where the others were waiting impatiently.

"Where have you been?" Lisa asked.

"I was looking through the dresses in the back," Kelly said.

"That's funny. Jessie looked there," Zack said.

Just then Jessie walked up. "There you are, Kelly! Have you seen Slater?"

"Uh, is he missing?" Kelly asked.

"He's right here," Slater said, walking up. "I was checking out the roof."

"Well, now that we're all here, let's get a move on," Zack said.

Willy looked up from where he was straightening his desk. "Are you sure you don't want to help me clean up?" he asked, a mischievous twinkle in his brown eyes.

"Thanks, anyway," Zack said. "We've got our own mess to deal with."

"Where's my necklace?" Jessie asked Slater. "I want to put it back on."

"Oh, sure," Slater said. He reached into his pocket. "Oh, my gosh," he said. He drew out his pocket and showed her the hole. "It must have dropped out!"

"It couldn't have!" Jessie said, aghast. "Slater, we have to find it!"

"We don't have time," Zack said. "We have to get back to Bayside. We're really cutting it close now."

Jessie was almost crying. "But I can't leave without it! I love it."

"I'll keep an eye out for it while I'm cleaning up," Willy told her. "I'll mail it to you. I promise."

Jessie still looked reluctant to go. She scanned the floorboards anxiously. "Can't we just look for it now?"

"Jessie, we really have to go," Zack said firmly. "Lisa is going to be in big trouble if we don't switch those dresses."

"All right," Jessie said slowly. "I guess you're right."

The gang said good-bye to Willy and filed out

the door. Slater and Kelly exchanged a relieved glance. They were safe!

But halfway down the stairs, they heard a call. Willy's head popped over the railing high above. A glittering object dangled from his fingers.

"Jessie!" he yelled. "I found it!"

Chapter 8

▲ ▼ ▲ ▼ ▲

Everyone else waited in the parking lot while Zack and Lisa switched the dresses. Lisa and Zack ran out of school and hurriedly tossed a bag with the stained dress in it onto the backseat of Zack's Mustang.

"Let's go over the plan again," Kelly suggested.

"Good idea," Screech said. "Now, what do I do after I bring the salami to the museum?"

"Not the salami, Screech, the *Origami*," Lisa said impatiently. "You and Zack will bring the dress to the museum and stash it in the coat check. Meanwhile—"

"We'll all sneak into the party as waiters," Slater said.

"And then we'll get some trays of food," Zack continued. "We have to find something green and yucky so it will match the stain on the Origami. Then all we have to do is spill it on Mrs. Belding from behind."

"So that she won't see us," Jessie added. "We don't want Mr. Belding to be mad at us."

"Then we'll offer to help her," Zack continued. "Jessie will say she has a great spot cleaner in her knapsack. She'll get the dress from Mrs. B., and Lisa will loan her an outfit to wear while she waits. Then we'll switch the dresses and give the Origami back to Mrs. B. instead of the Kozinski. Jessie will say the stain wouldn't come out. Mrs. B. won't notice the difference because the stain will look the same."

"Do you think it will work?" Kelly asked, frowning. "It sounds so complicated."

"What choice do we have?" Lisa said.

"Well, we could tell the truth," Kelly said.

Zack gave her an incredulous look. "Kelly, why should we tell the truth when this scam might work?"

That's just the trouble, Zack, Kelly wanted to say. *Telling the truth never occurs to you.*

"Are you in or out, Kelly?" Lisa asked anxiously. "Because we really need you."

"Of course I'm in," Kelly said. "I wouldn't let you guys down."

"That's my girl," Zack said.

At his words, Kelly gave him a weird, uneasy smile. *As soon as this is over,* Zack thought, *Kelly and I had better have a talk.* Something was definitely wrong between them. But it was nothing that a romantic night at the beach couldn't cure. He just had to get Kelly alone and tell her how much he loved her.

"Okay, are we all set?" Jessie said. "We'd better get moving. We have to be at Mr. Belding's soon."

"Right," Zack said, tearing his gaze away from Kelly. "Everyone dress in black pants and a white shirt and meet at the Max in half an hour. Then we'll all stop off at the Beldings like we promised. Don't forget your camera, Jessie."

"And let's hope that Mrs. B. doesn't have as good an eye for fashion as Lisa," Kelly added.

"I don't think there's much chance of *that*," Lisa said with a sniff.

▲   ▼   ▲

Kelly was the first one to arrive at the Max. She slid into the gang's usual booth and ordered an iced tea. She'd dressed in half her usual time just in case Slater would be early, too. She was hoping that he had the same idea as she did.

But she nearly choked on her straw when Jessie strode through the door in a crisp white shirt and black jeans. The silver locket swung with the motion of Jessie's long-legged, impatient walk.

"Are we the first ones here?" she asked Kelly, looking around the Max.

Kelly nodded. "The guys will never believe that we got ready before they did," she said, trying to joke.

Jessie slid into the booth. "Don't take this personally, Kelly, but I was kind of hoping Slater would be here instead of you. I really wanted to see him alone."

Kelly stirred her iced tea. "It's okay. I understand."

Jessie leaned back against the booth with a sigh. "I'm not blind. I know that things are rocky between us. I know that I've let him down. I hurt him, and he's afraid if we get together again, for good this time, I might do it again. He's just scared, that's all. I have to admit that I was nervous that we'd *never* get back what we had."

Jessie fingered the locket, a smile stealing over her face. Kelly saw nervously that Jessie's fingers were very near the catch.

"How do you feel now?" she asked. She didn't want to keep talking about this, but she was so afraid that Jessie would spring the locket catch by mistake!

"Oh, I think there's definitely hope," Jessie said. "Obviously, Slater wants to try. That's why this pendant means so much to me. It's a symbol of our love. Even when we were at our most distant, Slater went out and bought me this. That's the thing about our relationship, Kelly. No matter what happens, I know that I'm the special girl in Slater's life. Even when he was dating other people, I knew it. And when we got back together, he told me so himself."

"What did he tell you?" Kelly asked. She really didn't want to hear the answer, but she couldn't help herself.

"That I'm the only girl for him," Jessie said, her eyes dreamy. "And that I always will be."

"When did he say that?" Kelly said. "After Santa Fe?"

Jessie looked uncomfortable. "Well, no. It was a couple of months ago. But things haven't changed, Kelly. No matter what we go through, we always end up together. We have this chemical attraction. When we get together, *boom*!" Jessie clapped her hands together. "I'll always love Slater, and he'll always love me. It's as simple as that."

Kelly didn't say anything. She didn't know what to say. She felt so guilty she couldn't talk, anyway.

Luckily, Jessie didn't notice her silence. She was staring dreamily into space. "It's just fate, I guess. And I'm going to try my hardest to make Slater happy from now on. I'm going to be sweet and loving and supportive. I know that we argue too much. But if I make an effort, things will change. After all, we've been there for each other time and time again. We can't turn our backs on that." Jessie looked at Kelly. "Don't you feel the same way about Zack?" she asked.

Kelly opened her mouth, but no sound came out.

"Kelly?" Jessie asked. "Are you okay?"

Just then, the door burst open, and in walked Zack and Slater. Kelly blinked at them as though she'd never seen them before. Zack was blond and slender. Slater was dark and muscular. Zack was the life of every party. Slater liked to sit in a corner and watch. Zack courted trouble. Slater wanted to cruise through life.

She knew Zack inside and out. But Slater was still a bit of a mystery. Maybe that was what was so intriguing and challenging about him.

Kelly felt as though her heart would burst on the spot. She really did love them both. So which one was the boy for her? And was she willing to break her best friend's heart to find out?

▲　▼　▲

Mr. Belding greeted them at the door to his house, beaming a happy smile. He was dressed in a tuxedo with a snowy white shirt and a satin cummerbund.

"How do I look?" he asked.

"Very nice," Kelly said.

"I approve," Lisa said, slowly circling the tux. "*Very* elegant."

"Not too elegant, I hope," Mr. Belding said, straightening his bow tie. He leaned over and murmured, "I don't want to outshine Mrs. B."

Jessie bit her lip to keep from laughing. "I don't think you will," she whispered.

"Are you ready, honey? The kids are here with the camera," Mr. Belding called up the stairs.

"I'm ready," Mrs. Belding said. "But, oh, I'm so nervous." She stood at the top of the stairs in Willy Kozinski's dark blue satin gown.

Lisa sucked in her breath. If she didn't know better, she'd think the dress *was* an Origami. Willy was right. He was a genius. Or maybe it was the lighting.

Mrs. Belding came slowly down the stairs.

"That's an incredibly beautiful dress," Jessie said.

"It's an Origami, isn't it," Lisa said.

"An Origami! Oh, darling!" Mrs. Belding said to Mr. Belding. "I didn't realize! I mean, I knew it was beautiful, but . . . How extravagant!"

"Mr. Belding, I just knew you had perfect taste," Lisa beamed approvingly.

"W-well, um, thank you, Lisa," Mr. Belding stammered. "Darling, you look beautiful."

"Origami is my favorite designer, Mrs. B.," Lisa said. "You're going to knock 'em dead."

Mrs. Belding smoothed her hands over the dress. "I couldn't believe it when I opened the garment bag. Just wait until Amanda Stiffington, the head of the docent committee, sees this! I never dreamed I'd own something so gorgeous!"

"The woman makes the dress, Mrs. B.," Zack said. "You look beautiful."

"Thank you, Zack. That's really sweet. I just hope I don't spill anything on it. I'm kind of a klutz, you know," Mrs. Belding admitted, smiling. "Maybe you'd better take our picture now."

Mr. and Mrs. Belding stood in front of the fireplace while Jessie snapped off several shots. After a few minutes, Mr. Belding looked at his watch. "Time to go, dear. We don't want to be late."

"We'll see you there," Zack said. "We all got jobs with the caterer to pick up some extra money."

"Yeah, thanks for the tip, Mr. B.," Slater said.

Mr. Belding looked uneasy. "That's great, gang. But be careful around Mrs. B., will you? I wouldn't want anything to happen to that dress."

Screech gasped. "How did you—"

"Get your hair in that French twist?" Lisa interrupted quickly as she admired Mrs. Belding's hairdo.

"My secret is lots of hair spray," Mrs. B. said.

Mr. Belding helped Mrs. Belding on with her wrap. "We really have to get going," he said. "Thanks for dropping by and taking pictures, gang."

"Don't mention it, Mr. B.," Zack said.

"Well, good-bye then," Mr. Belding said as

they all left the house. "And remember," he called over his shoulder as he headed for the car, "don't spill anything on Mrs. Belding tonight!"

The gang all laughed a bit too loudly. "Us?" Zack said. "You've got to be kidding, Mr. Belding. We'd never spill a thing!"

"Gosh," Lisa said. "I hope we can get into the museum."

"We've come this far," Zack said. "Nothing can stop us now."

Chapter 9

▲   ▼   ▲   ▼   ▲

The museum was still open when they arrived, so they simply paid the admission charge and walked in. They followed directions to the members' private dining room on the fourth floor. There was a coat check to the right of the door, where Zack quickly checked Mrs. Belding's Origami dress. Then they just walked into the private dining room.

"Whew. This was easy," Zack said in relief.

But they'd only taken two steps when a tall, impatient-looking man with red hair stopped them.

"Who are you, and what are you doing here?"

"We're with the caterer," Zack answered quickly, flashing the man a friendly smile.

"Oh, really? That's interesting. Seeing that I'm the manager on this job. And I have no idea what you're doing here."

"We're extra staff," Zack said.

"But I'm the one who orders extra staff," the man said with a grim smile. "And I *didn't* order any."

Kelly stepped forward. "Mrs. Stiffington did," she said. The name had just floated into her head. Hadn't Mrs. Belding wanted to prove herself to Amanda Stiffington? That must mean that Mrs. Stiffington was a big deal.

The redheaded man let out an annoyed breath. "Not Mrs. Stiffington again."

Kelly smiled sympathetically. "She called the office and demanded extra staff. She started to freak because she imagined people having to wait more than ten seconds for an hors d'oeuvre."

The man rolled his eyes. "Tell me about it."

"I'm Kelly," Kelly said. "You must be . . . "

"Rusty."

"Right. Rusty. They told us to ask for you."

Rusty nodded. "Okay, kids, head for the kitchen, second door on your right. Ask for

Chrissie. We're going to start serving in about five minutes, after the museum closes. So look sharp."

Kelly and the gang dashed off. "I can't believe this," Zack said. "Kelly, you're brilliant."

"You can't believe that Kelly is brilliant?" Slater asked, a tinge of irritation in his voice.

"That's not what I meant," Zack said. "Kelly, you're turning out to be my main challenger for the scam meister title of Bayside High."

"I didn't know you had it in you," Jessie said.

"I did," Slater said gruffly. "Kelly can do anything."

"I know that," Zack said.

Slater scowled, and Jessie looked at him quizzically. Why was Slater so irritated with Zack? She'd caught him shooting Zack dirty looks all day long.

But she didn't have time to puzzle it out. As soon as they reached the bustling service area, they were given long white aprons by a cheerful girl named Chrissie. Chrissie quickly ran through the schedule of how the food would be served.

"Let me get this straight," Lisa murmured nervously. "First, the hot shrimp puffs. Then, quail eggs. After that, the baked brie."

"No, the brie comes before the quail eggs," Kelly corrected. "I think."

"And you forgot the saucisson en croûte," Jessie reminded them.

"I don't understand all these fancy foods," Slater grumbled. "Why can't they just serve pigs in a blanket?"

"That *is* pigs in a blanket," Jessie said, giggling.

"It doesn't matter, anyway," Zack said, popping up behind them. "All we have to worry about is the spinach liver pâté."

"Why do we have to worry about it?" Screech asked. "Leave it to the chef. We have enough to worry about. At least I do. I have to carry this tray through a roomful of people in fancy clothes without dropping it."

"Exactly my point, Screech," Zack said. He held up a container. "Except that we *want* you to drop it. Take a good look at this, guys."

Lisa leaned over. "Yuck," she sniffed. "That stuff looks like the bottom of my parakeet's cage."

"It smells like it, too," Slater said.

"Exactly," Zack said happily. "Look at that putrid greenish brown color. Remind you of anything?"

"The stain!" everybody said together.

"It will definitely match," Lisa said excitedly.

"I have more good news," Zack said. "I just

heard that they're going to show a short clip from a film on the artist who's having a retrospective here next month. When the lights go down, it will be a perfect opportunity to spill this on Mrs. Belding. She won't see a thing!"

"It looks like fate is on our side," Lisa said happily. "What could go wrong?"

"Battle stations, everyone," Zack said, picking up a tray.

Kelly hoisted her own tray up. "Oof," she said.

"Let me take that, Kelly," Slater said quickly. "It's too heavy for you."

"No, I'm okay," Kelly said with a strained smile.

"I insist," Slater said. "Take that other tray instead. Here," he said, reaching out for her tray.

"I'll take it, Slater," Zack said, grabbing the edge of it.

"I've got it, Zack," Slater said firmly.

"I'll take it," Zack insisted. "She's *my* girl-friend. I can take it if it's too heavy for her."

"Well, then maybe you should have noticed it first," Slater said evenly. "But that wouldn't be like you, would it, Zack?"

"Hey, you guys," Kelly said nervously. "Cut it out. Stop arguing."

Jessie looked at Slater curiously. Why was he

making a big deal out of this? Besides, her tray was just as heavy as Kelly's. "Somebody had better let go," she advised. "Or the whole thing is going to—"

Crash!

Everybody looked down at the pile of food and dishware on the floor.

"Great," Jessie said. "Now we'll get fired before we even start working."

"This even breaks *my* record for holding a job," Zack said.

"No, I think it's just dishes," Screech observed. "I don't see any records down there. Besides, the sound system uses tapes, I think."

"We'd better clean it up—fast," Lisa urged in a low tone.

"I'll do it," Zack said. "There's no sense you all getting in trouble, too. You guys better disappear."

Everyone started to scatter while Zack went off in search of a broom. Slater tugged at Kelly's elbow. "Come on. Didn't you hear him?" he said.

"What do you want to do?" Kelly asked.

Slater grinned. "Disappear. Haven't I ever shown you my favorite painting?" Taking her hand, he pulled her through a door.

▲   ▼   ▲

Slater led Kelly through the deserted museum galleries. They raced breathlessly through one after another. The paintings were a blur of color against the white walls as Kelly felt Slater tug her along, his hand warm and strong in hers.

Finally he came to a stop. "I think we're far enough away now," he said.

"But won't they miss us?" Kelly asked nervously.

"No way. That room is too crowded," Slater said. "And they'll be too busy passing shrimp puffs."

Kelly cast a nervous look backward. "But they need us."

"Not yet," Slater said. "Not until the film goes on. And why should we slave away serving fancy French pigs in a blanket to a bunch of people we don't even know?"

Kelly laughed. "Good point. I do enough serving at the Yogurt 4-U."

"And I really wanted to talk to you, Kelly," Slater said. "First of all, I'm sorry about that scene before. I acted like a jerk, I guess."

"It's okay," Kelly said. "So did Zack."

"I just get so mad at him," Slater said. "He

doesn't really see you, Kelly. He only thinks about himself sometimes."

"That's not fair, Slater," Kelly said. "He's trying to help Lisa right now."

"I guess you're right," Slater said. "Maybe I'm just jealous."

"That's okay," Kelly said. "When Jessie was talking about you at the Max, I wanted to stick my straw up her nose."

Slater and Kelly burst out laughing.

"Then I guess we're both guilty," Slater said.

"We are both guilty, Slater," Kelly said, suddenly serious. "I know I feel guilty. Don't you?"

Slater nodded slowly. "I do."

Kelly dropped Slater's hand and moved away a few steps. "So does that mean that we're doing something wrong?"

Slater opened his mouth to assure her that it didn't. But instead, he sighed. "I don't know," he said, feeling helpless.

"I think it does," Kelly said quietly. "I don't like feeling guilty, Slater. I don't like hiding things from the rest of the gang. An inscription in a locket or my feelings."

"What are you saying, Kelly?" Slater asked. It was funny how steady his voice sounded, he thought. Because his heart was thumping like the huge drum in the Bayside marching band.

"That maybe we should forget this," Kelly said in a small voice. "Is it really worth hurting Jessie and Zack?" She turned to him, her blue eyes troubled. "I talked to Jessie. She's willing to really work at your relationship."

"I don't want to *work* at a relationship," Slater said, frustrated. "That's just the trouble with Jessie. She treats life like a term paper. The last time we had a 'relationship talk,' she took notes! Everything with her is hard work. And everything with you is so easy."

"Did you ever think," Kelly said, "that the reason it's easy is because we don't know each other as well? I mean, we know each other as friends. But when you start to date someone, it's a whole new ball game."

"Maybe you're right," Slater said. "But that still doesn't mean I have to stay with Jessie."

"Slater, she loves you so much," Kelly said.

"I know," Slater said.

"And I love Jessie, too," Kelly said. "She's my best friend. I don't want to hurt her."

"I don't want to hurt Zack, either," Slater said.

"So that's that," Kelly said. "We have no choice. We have to do what's right."

"Not see each other," Slater said. "But what if Jessie and I *do* break up?"

Kelly swallowed. "It doesn't matter. I still won't go out with you, Slater. I couldn't look Jessie in the face if I did. Because I know how much she still cares about you. And I couldn't hurt Zack that way, either."

Slater wanted to punch a hole in the wall. He wanted to grab Kelly by the shoulders and tell her she was wrong. But he couldn't.

Because she was right.

Kelly saw all the tension drain out of Slater. He wasn't going to argue with her. Part of her was disappointed. But another part of her knew it was for the best.

"You're right, Kelly," he said finally. "Maybe we have to let something important go so we can keep something more important that we already have. Trust."

"I guess I could face losing Zack's love," Kelly said. "But I couldn't face losing his trust."

"I know what you mean," Slater said. "If Jessie and I break up, I want to stay friends. We've done it before. We can do it again. But not if I'm dating her best friend."

"So we say good-bye—right here," Kelly said.

Slater took a few steps toward her. He slipped

his arms around her in a hug. "Good-bye, Kelly. I'll really miss what I almost had with you."

Kelly tried to smile, but her lower lip wobbled. She hid her face in Slater's shoulder as her eyes filled with tears. "Good-bye," she whispered.

▲ ▼ ▲

Back at the party, Jessie sidled up to Zack with an empty tray. "Have you seen Slater?"

Zack shook his head. "Not in about fifteen minutes. I haven't seen Kelly, either."

"I hope those two aren't goofing off while we're doing all the dirty work," Lisa said.

"It would be just like Slater," Zack said. "He said if he wanted to be a waiter, he would have majored in serving food, not eating it."

"He's probably scarfing down shrimp puffs in the kitchen," Jessie said. "Or maybe he grabbed a plate of food and found a quiet place to eat it. I'm going to look for him."

"And find Kelly, too, while you're at it," Zack called after her. "We need all the help we can get."

Chapter 10

▲ ▼ ▲ ▼ ▲

Zack grabbed his freshened tray and started out toward the party again. But before he could enter the crowded room, a large hand descended on his shoulder.

"It's too early for the pâté," Rusty told him. "Didn't Chrissie tell you the schedule? We're still circulating the saucisson and the baked brie."

"Sorry," Zack said, sliding his tray back on the service station. "I thought the brie was, uh, brie-ed out."

"Ask Chrissie for another tray," Rusty instructed as he hurried past. "And keep those trays circulating!"

Zack headed back toward Chrissie grumpily.

It was a total drag having to work and not even get paid! As soon as he was able to dump the gunk on Mrs. B., he was grabbing Kelly's hand and heading to the Max for some good old American french fries.

He saw Lisa filling her tray and went over to her. "The sooner we get rid of this brie, the sooner we can get out the pâté," he murmured. "So pass it around. Rusty is watching me like a hawk, and the film clip is coming up soon."

Lisa nodded. "I wish Mrs. B. would move," she said. "She's glued to that seat with her back to the wall. I don't know how we're going to get close without her seeing us."

Zack sighed as he filled his tray with bite-size pieces of cheese wrapped in pastry. How was he going to blast Mrs. B. out of that chair? She had turned out to be awfully shy. She looked completely intimidated by the fancy museum crowd. Meanwhile, Mr. Belding looked as if he'd been stuffed and mounted against the wall. He belonged in a natural history museum, not an art museum.

"Excuse me. Are these those yummy little brie puffs?" The tall, elegant woman by Zack's side spoke in a Texas twang.

"Yes, ma'am," Zack said distractedly. He held out the tray toward her.

"I'll have to spend an extra twenty minutes tomorrow on that torture device—that stationary bicycle contraption—but who cares," the woman said, taking a bite of pastry. Her blue eyes shined at Zack. "Besides," she said, "eating these sure beats standing alone in a corner."

"Excuse me, ma'am," Zack said. "I don't mean to pry or anything. But is this your first museum party?"

She nodded. "Just moved here from Dallas. My Hank was supposed to come along tonight, but he had a meeting. So I figured what could be so scary about a roomful of L.A. swells? Rosie Ruskin—that's me—threw the biggest, bestest barbecues in all of Rabbit Foot County, Texas. But here's a news flash for you, handsome. Turns out I'm terrified."

Zack had an inspiration. "I'll give you a tip," he said, placing two more brie puffs on her napkin. "You see that woman in the blue dress sitting in the corner over there?"

"The one in that Origami? Sure."

"This is her first party, too. And she looks pretty scared herself."

The tall woman peered across the room. "She does, poor thing. Maybe I should mosey on over and chat her up a spell."

Zack handed her another cheese puff. "I think that would be an excellent idea."

Popping a cheese puff into her mouth, Rosie Ruskin made her way across the room. Zack watched in satisfaction as she leaned over to say hello to Mrs. Belding. Mrs. B. stood up when she was introduced and began laughing at something the woman from Texas said. As Zack watched, Mr. Belding joined in, and in another moment they had moved away from the wall.

"Good work," Lisa said as she slipped by him. "How'd you manage that one?"

"Put two wallflowers together and you can make a party," Zack said. "I'm all out of cheese puffs. And the movie's about to start. It's time to mobilize our forces."

▲   ▼   ▲

A few minutes later, Zack, Screech, and Lisa all had trays full of spinach pâté. They lined up and faced the roomful of guests. Mrs. Belding, Mr. Belding, and Rosie Ruskin were still laughing and talking.

"She's pretty distracted," Lisa murmured. "Maybe this is a good time."

"Let's give it a shot," Zack said.

The three split up and made their way through the crowd. But by the time they'd made it halfway through the room, their trays were empty.

"Who knew this green slime would be so popular?" Lisa grumbled as she returned to the waiters' service station.

"I had a feeling," Screech said.

"It figures," Lisa said. "You like peanut-butter-and-pickle sandwiches."

"Don't forget the crushed potato chips," Screech said. "That's the crucial ingredient."

Just then Amanda Stiffington clapped her hands for silence.

"Attention, ladies and gentlemen," she called in her throaty voice. "We have a special treat for you this evening. It's a short excerpt from the film we'll be showing about Rodolfo Guitaras, the subject of our next retrospective here at the museum. As we all know, Guitaras was one of the founding members of the school of optic nervism."

"Of course," Lisa murmured. "We knew that."

"The lights, please," Mrs. Stiffington called.

"Here we go, gang," Zack murmured.

"Where are Kelly, Slater, and Jessie?" Lisa asked, twisting around.

"Never mind," Zack said as the lights went out. "Just go."

"Wait!" Lisa cried. "My tray is empty."

"So's mine," Screech whispered.

"Hurry up," Zack said, reaching to load their trays with plates of spinach pâté. "The film is starting."

As soon as they all had full trays, they split up again and moved toward the corner of the room where Mrs. Belding was standing. A man reached out for a scoop of pâté from Zack's tray, but Zack deftly moved aside.

"Sorry," he whispered. "This tray is reserved for Mrs. Stiffington."

"The whole tray?" the man asked incredulously.

"Why do you think she's the boss?" Zack asked. A woman near Lisa held up a finger to stop her. "Excuse me," she said. "I'd just love more of that pâté."

Lisa quickly surveyed the woman's tight gold brocade dress. "Are you sure, honey?" she said. "If you have any more, I don't think your seams are going to hold."

The woman gasped, and Lisa began to move past her, her eyes on Mrs. Belding's back.

Screech was having troubles of his own. A burly, bald man blocked his path. "My favorite!" he said, reaching for the whole plate of goop.

Screech quickly shook his head. "I wouldn't if I were you," he whispered. "Ptomaine city."

"I'm from Yuba City, myself," the man said jovially. "We must be neighbors!"

While Screech tried to ease away from the friendly man, Zack reached Mrs. Belding. He came up behind Mr. and Mrs. Belding and pitched his voice very low.

"Pâté, madam?" As he spoke, he began to tilt his tray so that the plate of green glop began to slide forward.

Mrs. Belding half turned, her eyes still on the movie screen. "No, thank you."

The plate of pâté hung on the edge of the tray. Any minute now, it would slide right onto the front of Mrs. B's dress. . . .

"Whoa, watch out, young feller!"

To Zack's annoyance, Rosie Ruskin reached out and tipped the tray back to a level position.

"You almost wore that green goop home," she whispered to Mrs. Belding. "That waiter is friendly, but I bet his name isn't Grace!"

"Which waiter?" Mr. Belding asked, but Zack had already stepped back behind the curtains. He waited there until the three had turned around and looked at the screen again.

"Darn," he murmured under his breath. Now it was up to Lisa and Screech. Peeking around the curtain, he saw that Lisa was tied up with a woman in a formfitting gold dress. The woman had dragged Rusty over and was shaking her finger at him and Lisa. Zack guessed that Lisa was about to lose her first catering job.

He looked over at the opposite end of the room for Screech. But just then the short film ended, and Zack saw in despair that Screech was too far away. Any minute now, the lights would go up. "Lights!" Mrs. Stiffington called. But the lights stayed out.

"Lights!" Mrs. Stiffington called again.

Suddenly Zack realized that he was standing by the light switch. A guard rushed over to flick the switch. The lights flooded on.

"Ah—" Mrs. Stiffington said. "Now—"

Zack reached over and flicked the lights off again. "*Go,*" he murmured to Screech.

But now he saw that Lisa had made her way across the room. She was right behind Screech, who was trying to free himself from a bald man who was slapping him on the back.

Lisa came to a dead halt behind a group of people who were discussing optic nervism. She nudged a woman out of the way with the end of her tray. What did she care? Rusty had already fired her!

The woman stepped back, right on Lisa's brand-new suede shoes. "Hey!" Lisa protested, turning. "Watch it!"

But as she turned, her tray bonked Screech on the back of the head. Screech was off balance as he tried to move away from the bald man, and he went flying. He tripped over someone's legs, then a chair, and finally fell to the floor, right on his pointed chin.

Lisa couldn't believe her good luck. Screech's tray left his hands and flew right onto Mrs. Belding!

Chapter 11

▲ ▼ ▲ ▼ ▲

Mrs. Belding screamed. Mr. Belding clutched his head in horror. Rosie Ruskin clucked her tongue.

The guard switched on the lights again, and Zack eased out from behind the curtain. Screech crawled away through a forest of legs before anyone could finger him as the culprit.

"My dress!" Mrs. Belding wailed.

"Did anyone see who that was?" Rusty demanded.

"It was that young waiter from Ptomaine City, I think," the bald man said.

Lisa hurried forward. "Oh, Mrs. B.," she said. "What a terrible stain."

"You might want to try some club soda," Rosie Ruskin said sympathetically. "Works like a charm on my own special fire-breathing hot sauce."

"Come with me, Mrs. B.," Lisa said, leading her and Mr. Belding through the crowd.

She found Jessie waiting in the hall. "Oh, Mrs. B., I'm so sorry," Jessie said. "Your beautiful dress."

Mrs. Belding tried to smile. "Maybe it will come out."

"I have an idea," Jessie said. "I have some stain remover in my knapsack. I, uh, used it in home ec."

"And I wore my sweat suit here," Lisa told her. "Why don't you slip out of the dress in the ladies' room and change into my sweats? We're the same size."

"How do you know that, Lisa?" Mrs. B. asked.

Lisa swallowed nervously. "Well, I'm guessing. But you'll definitely fit into my sweats. There's a nice waiting room in the ladies' room. Jessie and I will take the dress and try to get out the stain at the waiters' station. It will only take five minutes or so."

"Do you think that's what we should do?" Mrs. Belding asked worriedly. "Maybe I should just take it to the Origami store on Monday."

"No, don't do that," Mr. Belding said, speaking up for the first time. "Let's first see if the girls can help."

Lisa and Jessie led Mrs. Belding into the ladies' room. Mrs. B. went into a stall to change. She handed the dress over the partition.

"We'll be right back," Jessie called as she and Lisa hurried out.

Zack was waiting by the coat check with Mrs. Belding's original dress. He had poured some water on it to make the stain damp. Now it looked exactly like the Willy Kozinski. "Here," he said, thrusting it at Lisa and Jessie.

"We did it!" he exulted. "Isn't it great?"

"I guess so," Lisa said.

"Mrs. B. is really upset," Jessie said.

"She was almost crying," Lisa said. "I feel really guilty. She finally gets a designer dress, and it's ruined."

"It might not be ruined," Zack said. "After you tell her you can't get the stain out, she'll probably take it back to Origami's. Maybe he can fix it or something."

"That's true," Lisa said, brightening.

"The only difference is, this way it won't be your fault," Zack said. "Come on, Lisa. We've all gone to a heap of trouble for you. The least you can do is be happy."

"I am happy," Lisa said. "I guess."

"Come on," Jessie said. "Let's take the dress back to Mrs. B."

They hurried back to the ladies' room, where Mrs. Belding was sitting on the pink couch, sadly fluffing out her light brown hair.

"I'm sorry, Mrs. B.," Jessie said, holding out the dress. "We couldn't get it out."

"I'm *really* sorry," Lisa said fervently. "Really, really sorry. You can't believe how sorry I am."

Mrs. Belding smiled wanly. "It's not your fault, Lisa," she said.

"Well, it's just that, you know, I love clothes so much," Lisa said, stroking the dress. "And this is such a beautiful dress."

Mrs. Belding stood up. "Well, Mr. B. and I might as well head home. We weren't having a very good time, anyway. I only met one person I liked. Lisa, can I wear your sweat suit home? Mr. B. can bring it to school on Monday."

"Of course, Mrs. Belding. You can have anything of mine you want," Lisa said. "Do you want my purse? It looks real cute with that outfit."

Mrs. Belding laughed. "No, thanks. Come on. Let's go give Mr. B. the bad news."

They walked outside, where Mr. Belding was waiting in the hall with Zack and Screech. "How is it?" he asked anxiously. "Did the stain come out?"

Mrs. Belding shook her head. "I'm afraid not, hon." She surveyed everyone's faces. "Hey, you guys. I hate to break it to you, but it's just a dress. My dog didn't die or anything. I'll survive."

"I'm really, really sorry, Mrs. B.," Lisa said again.

"Maybe the Origami store will have some suggestions on how to get it out," Zack said.

"That's right," Lisa said. "Antonio Origami stands behind his clothes."

"Why does he stand behind them?" Screech asked. "He'll never get any publicity that way. No one will see him."

Lisa rolled her eyes. "Anyway, you should go to the store on Monday, Mrs. B."

"I will," Mrs. Belding said, folding the dress over her arm.

Zack saw Mr. Belding gulp.

"Coming, dear?" Mrs. B. said.

"In a minute," Mr. Belding said. "I'll meet you by the elevators."

As soon as Mrs. Belding was out of earshot, Mr. Belding turned to them. He looked desperate. "What am I going to do now?" he said.

"What do you mean, Mr. B.?" Zack asked.

"I have to come clean to you guys," Mr. Belding said.

"Did you get a stain, too?" Screech asked, horrified.

"No, I mean I have to confess something," Mr. Belding said. "I might need your help. That dress is *not* an original Origami. It's what they call a knockoff. It's made by this brilliant young designer. His name is—"

"*Willy Kozinski!*" Zack, Screech, Jessie, and Lisa cried.

"How did you know?" Mr. Belding said. He passed a hand over his forehead. "What am I going to do? I'm ruined."

"What am *I* going to do?" Lisa wailed. "It will be all over town now. My fashion eye is blind!"

"Or at least not twenty-twenty," Jessie said.

"Hold on a sec here," Zack said. He almost chortled in glee. He felt sorry for Mr. Belding, but he was also tickled pink. He'd spent many a long hour warming the seat in Mr. Belding's office because of a scam or a little white lie. He'd received so many lectures from Mr. Belding on the importance of telling the truth that he could recite them in his sleep. And now *he* had caught *Mr. Belding* in a lie!

"Let me get this straight," Zack said. "You *lied* to Mrs. Belding?"

"Just a little bit," Mr. Belding said uneasily.

"I'd say it was a whopper," Zack said.

"You don't understand," Mr. Belding said. "I was going to tell her it was a knockoff. And it was plenty expensive, anyway, let me tell you. But then Lisa and the girls just assumed it was an original Origami, and Mrs. B. was so happy. I just couldn't bear to set her straight. So I just . . . let her think it was. So you see, it wasn't really a lie," Mr. Belding finished. "Technically."

"Mr. Belding, you sound like Zack," Jessie said, amused.

Mr. Belding closed his eyes, as if in pain. "You're right," he said. He looked horrified. "Don't tell me he's rubbing off on me!"

"Just be glad he's not eating a hot dog," Screech said authoritatively. "Take it from us, mustard is hard to get out."

"I'm going to have to tell her the truth," Mr. Belding said with a sigh. He turned to them. "Thanks, you guys. I owe you big."

"You do?" Lisa asked incredulously.

"I've been feeling awful all evening," Mr. Belding admitted. "I'd never lied to Mrs. B. before. That dress was coming between us. I'm glad it got stained. It taught me a valuable lesson. Always tell the truth. Even when you're afraid you'll upset someone you love. Chances are, they'll understand."

"And chances are, they'll find out, anyway," Zack said. "That's always been my experience."

"Mr. Belding, don't worry," Lisa said. "I think Mrs. Belding will really be touched that you were trying to please her."

"I hope so. And I'll never forget the favor you all did for me tonight," Mr. Belding said. "Thanks, gang."

"You're welcome," the four of them said weakly.

"I still feel kind of guilty," Lisa said after Mr. Belding had gone.

"Why, Lisa?" Zack asked. "You saved Mr. Belding's marriage!"

"Well, I know one thing," Lisa said as she whipped off her apron. "I'm out of here."

"Where are you going, Lisa?" Screech asked.

"Back to Willy's studio," Lisa said crisply. "If that guy can fool me, he must be a genius!"

"I'll drive you," Screech offered.

Jessie turned to Zack. "I looked all over for Slater and Kelly. They've been missing for ages."

"I think they went that way," Screech said,

pointing toward a door. "Slater said he wanted to show Kelly his favorite painting."

"*Slater* said that?" Jessie said, incredulous. "He doesn't know a painting from a . . . from a comic book!"

"I'm just saying what I heard," Screech said.

Lisa waved at Screech by the elevators. "Hurry up, Screech! I want to catch Willy before he leaves!"

"Sorry, you guys," Screech said. "My reason for living is calling. Hope you find Kelly and Slater." He rushed off, his springy curls bobbing.

"Maybe we should check it out," Zack said to Jessie. "Maybe they slipped away so they didn't have to serve at the party. I wish I had thought of that."

"Me, too," Jessie said, laughing. "Let's look ar—"

Suddenly she was interrupted by a loud clanging. A tall, lanky guard rushed past them down the corridor.

"What's going on?" Zack shouted.

"There's been a theft!" the guard yelled.

Zack and Jessie exchanged glances and then rushed after the guard. He opened the door into the museum galleries.

Zack and Jessie heard another guard speak

from the other side of the door. "Turn off that alarm, Larry! I caught them red-handed!"

"Wow," Jessie said to Zack. "Isn't this exciting?"

A second later, a beefy guard barreled through the doorway, pushing a couple ahead of him. Jessie and Zack gasped. It was Slater and Kelly!

Chapter 12

▲　▼　▲　▼　▲

"They aren't thieves!" Zack shouted.

"They're high school students!" Jessie protested.

"It's true," Slater told the beefy guard.

"We didn't steal anything," Kelly said pleadingly.

"Right," the guard said. "So do you mind telling me what you were doing in a museum gallery after closing time?"

"Looking at the paintings?" Slater asked.

"In the dark?" the lanky guard sneered.

"I have really good night vision," Slater said.

"So did you happen to see where the missing

painting went?" the beefy guard asked. "Because one's gone."

"A very *expensive* one," the lanky guard said. "Don't forget that, Ralph. It's grand larceny."

"I'm not forgetting it, Larry," the beefy guard said impatiently. "That's why I'm holding these two."

"We're with the caterer," Kelly said. "We just slipped away for a few minutes to, uh, get some air."

"In a stuffy old museum? Try another one," lanky Larry said.

The commotion had attracted some guests from the party. Rusty appeared at Zack's side. Zack seized his arm eagerly.

"Tell them, Rusty! Tell them that Kelly and Slater are working for you!"

"It's true," Rusty told the guards. "They are."

Ralph, the beefy guard, looked a little uncertain. "Have you worked with them often?"

"Well, no," Rusty said. "They were last-minute replacements. Mrs. Stiffington requested them."

"I did not!"

Zack and Jessie turned. Mrs. Stiffington was standing in the middle of the corridor. "I never

requested anyone," she said haughtily. "I don't
interfere with museum arrangements."

"Yeah, right," Rusty said under his breath.
But he turned to Zack and Jessie. "So if Mrs.
Stiffington didn't request you, what are you doing
here?" he asked.

Larry put a hand on his holster. "It's a gang! I
recognize that one!" he called shrilly, pointing at
Zack. "He's the one who kept switching off the
lights inside. It was a diversion!"

"And two of them are missing," Mrs. Stiffington added. "The weird-looking one with the
orange sneakers, and that pretty African-American
girl who told Muffy she needed to lose weight."

"They must have taken the painting with
them!" Larry cried.

"Uh-oh," Zack breathed.

Ralph hustled Slater and Kelly forward. He
gazed at Zack and Jessie with steely gray eyes.
"You'd better come with us."

▲   ▼   ▲

Ralph and Larry took Jessie, Zack, Slater, and
Kelly down in the service elevator to the security
office in the basement. While they glided down-
ward, the foursome tried to explain what they had
been doing in the museum.

"Wait," Ralph said. "Whose dress?"

"I think I've heard of Origami," Larry said. "Didn't we do a big blockbuster exhibition of his work last spring, Ralph?"

"No, Larry. That was Caravaggio. What was that about the spinach goop?" Ralph asked.

"We had to spill it on our principal's wife's designer dress," Lisa explained again. "And Screech did it. It was incredible, really."

"And he only has a mild concussion," Zack joked.

"You guys actually pulled it off?" Kelly asked. "Wow, that's amazing."

"How did Mrs. B. take it?" Slater asked.

"She was upset, but she's okay," Jessie said.

"Everything worked out great," Zack said. "We even saved Mr. B.'s marriage."

"Excuse me!" Ralph said pointedly.

"The least you could do is act a little bit scared," Larry said. "This is my first arrest. And that was the most unbelievable story I ever heard. If you ask me, Ralph, these guys need art heist lessons." He laughed a honking laugh.

Ralph closed his eyes. "Larry, please. Put a sock in it, will you?"

The elevator doors opened, and Larry and Ralph ushered them into the security office.

Another guard sat at a desk, watching the television monitors.

"What are you going to do now?" Jessie asked nervously.

"I'm going to find out the truth," Ralph said. "There's a real easy way to prove if you guys stole that painting. We'll just back up the tape about twenty minutes."

"You can't do that!" Slater exclaimed. He knew if Jessie and Zack saw the tape, they'd see him and Kelly kissing each other good-bye. And it had been a pretty long good-bye.

"Sure we can," Larry said.

"Can our friends wait outside?" Kelly asked. "They didn't have anything to do with it."

"Who said?" Larry said. "They're probably in on the whole heist."

"Pipe down, Larry," Ralph said. "Let's watch the tape. Al, run number three camera back twenty minutes, will you?"

Slater shot Kelly a panicked glance. Al punched a button, and an image of the empty gallery popped up on screen. Then Slater and Kelly walked in.

"There you are!" Jessie said.

"Kelly, you look great on TV," Zack said.

"Do you guys *mind*?" Ralph said.

Slater and Kelly watched themselves talk. There was no audio, so Zack and Jessie didn't know what they were saying. But any minute now, Slater would reach out and hug Kelly. Kelly would put her head on his shoulder. And then he would bend down, and she would tilt her head up, and they would kiss.

On the screen, Slater reached out to Kelly.

"Hey," Jessie said.

Slater bent down. Kelly tilted her head up.

"What—" Zack said.

"I had something in my eye," Kelly said quickly.

"When are you guys going to steal the painting?" Larry asked feverishly.

On the desk next to Ralph, a phone began to shrill. "Pause the tape a sec, Al," Ralph said.

The image of Slater bending over Kelly froze.

"It really hurt," Kelly said. "Wow."

"It was this big black speck," Slater said.

Ralph listened to the phone. Then he held it away from his ear, and they all heard the sound of a squawking voice. Ralph said, "Yes sir. I understand," and hung up.

He turned to Larry. "We've got to let them go."

"What? They stole a painting! There's a blank spot on the wall. Look!"

Ralph shook his head. "That was Harold Montepulciano on the phone. The curator. He heard what happened. He said the painting is gone for a cleaning. Looks like the kids were telling the truth."

"A cleaning?" Larry asked, disappointed. "But this was my first collar!"

"Sorry, Larry," Ralph said. He turned to the gang. "And sorry, kids. The museum owes you an apology. We'll give you some free passes to make up for it."

"It's okay," Kelly said. She was so relieved she felt like kissing Ralph. Zack and Jessie wouldn't see the rest of the tape!

"No problem," Slater said, shaking Ralph's hand.

Ralph looked from Kelly and Slater to Zack and Jessie. His gray eyes looked knowing, as if he had guessed why Kelly and Slater seemed extra relieved. "Good luck, kids. Remember, stay honest."

"Right," Slater gulped.

They filed out of the security office and took a deep breath.

"Whew," Zack said. "That was close."

"I thought we were going to spend the night in jail," Jessie said.

"It was our fault," Kelly said. "We shouldn't have disappeared like that."

"You missed all the fun," Jessie said.

"How's your eye now, Kelly?" Zack asked. "Are you okay?"

"Um, it feels fine," Kelly mumbled. She shot Slater a look from underneath her bangs. Their story had gone over so easily. There wasn't a doubt in anyone's mind that she really had had something in her eye.

But wasn't that why she and Slater were breaking things off? Because they just couldn't violate Zack and Jessie's trust?

"I'm sure glad I don't have to do any more catering," Jessie said, laughing as she began to untie her apron. She slipped it over her head, and her necklace chain caught in the strings. It popped off and fell to the floor.

"My necklace!" Jessie said, bending down on all fours to search for it in the dim light.

"Not again," Zack groaned.

"Oh, here it is!" Jessie said in relief. "It didn't go far." She stood up, clutching the necklace, and began to put it around her neck again.

But she stopped and peered at it. Kelly and Slater froze as her fingers ran over the tiny hinge on the pendant. They watched as Jessie sprang the catch and the pendant popped open.

"Hey," Jessie said, holding it up. "Look at this. It's not a pendant. It's a locket."

"Really?" Kelly squeaked.

Jessie looked closer at it. "And look at this, guys. There's an inscription!"

Chapter 13

▲ ▼ ▲ ▼ ▲

Slater took a step forward. "Jessie—"

"Did you know it had an inscription, Slater?" Jessie asked, peering at the locket. She held it up, trying to catch the light from behind her.

"It's too dark to read it in here," Slater said. "Let's go upstairs."

"Wait," Jessie said, peering at the locket. "I can just about make it out. Isn't this romantic?" she said to Kelly.

Kelly swallowed. "Um, I guess so."

"Just think," Jessie said dreamily. "Someone probably gave this locket to his sweetheart. Maybe even long ago. The catch was really hidden."

"Jessie, wait—" Slater said. "I need to talk to you. Alone."

"In a second," Jessie said absently, still peering at the locket. "Can you make this out, Zack?"

Zack leaned over. "*To K, Let's*—'"

"*'Let's begin,*'" Jessie read out excitedly. "And it's signed *'A.D.'* I wonder who *K* was. Katherine? Kimberly? Kristen? And *A.D.* . . . Alan . . . no, that's not romantic enough. I know—Alexander! And the second name is Dante. "*To Katherine, Let's begin. Alexander Dante.*'" Jessie sighed. "It *is* romantic!"

"Wait a second, Jessie," Zack said. "That's not a *D*. It's a *C*."

Slater and Kelly looked at each other helplessly.

"It's a *C*?" Jessie asked, disappointed. "Charles? Calvin? Why did it have to be a *C*? I don't like any *C* names. . . ." Suddenly Jessie stopped. Her hazel eyes widened. "A. *C*. A.C.," she said slowly.

"*To K,*'" Zack said.

Zack and Jessie stared at each other, openmouthed. "The tape!" they both said.

Slater and Kelly backed up a step. "L-let us explain," Slater stammered.

Jessie's eyes flashed. "Explain? Explain that

it's not to Katherine from Alexander Charles. It's to Kelly from A.C.! You were going to give this to *Kelly*, weren't you?"

"*My* Kelly!" Zack said. "But why?"

"And what does 'Let's begin' mean?" Jessie demanded.

"Begin what? Kelly, what's going on?" Zack asked. "And were you kissing on that tape, or not?"

Kelly and Slater exchanged a guilty look. Their nightmare was coming true. Zack and Jessie had found out—and in the worst possible way.

"We didn't mean for it to happen," Kelly said.

"Didn't mean for *what* to happen?" Zack asked.

"Are you two dating?" Jessie almost shrieked. "You're *seeing* each other?"

"Nothing's happened, really," Slater said. "We haven't even had a date, really."

"But obviously you're very close," Zack said icily.

"We spent a lot of time together in Santa Fe," Kelly said faintly. "And—"

"Not Santa Fe again!" Zack said. "Kelly, I told you I was sorry for what I did."

"I know you did, Zack," Kelly said quietly. "But did you really mean it?"

"And I apologized to you!" Jessie said to Slater. "You said you forgave me for turning our romantic weekend into my very own version of *Murder, She Wrote*. Now you're still punishing me for neglecting you?"

"Jessie, this isn't about punishing you," Slater said. "This is about what might be best for all of us."

"And about something we really couldn't control," Kelly said, spreading her hands. "Our feelings."

Jessie's voice shook. "Are you telling us that you guys are . . . are in love?"

"We don't know," Slater said. "How can we find out how we feel if we can never even be alone?"

Slater's words seemed to echo in the empty hallway. Jessie and Zack stood there as if they couldn't move a step if they tried. Kelly saw Zack swallow, and her eyes filled with tears. She couldn't stand to see the hurt and disbelief on his face.

"Zack, I'm so sorry," she whispered. She took a step toward him, but Zack took a step backward, shaking his head.

"How could you do this to me, Kelly?" Jessie asked. Tears glittered in her hazel eyes. "You're my best friend. How could you steal my boyfriend?"

"She didn't steal me," Slater said.

"I didn't mean to," Kelly said. "I mean, it just happened."

"And all the times I talked to you about him," Jessie said stormily. "You sat there listening, like you were my friend! You were laughing at me the whole time!"

"Jessie, I never laughed at you!" Kelly cried. "I felt awful!"

"We both did," Slater said.

"Like you were feeling *awful* in the gallery earlier?" Zack asked. "Or was it because your eye hurt so much, Kelly?"

"Zack, we were saying good-bye," Kelly said. "That's why we kissed. We'd decided not to think about each other anymore. We didn't want to hurt you and Jessie."

"Well, it's too late for that, isn't it!" Jessie said. She tossed her hair over her shoulder. "And why bother saying good-bye? You want to *begin*, don't you, Slater?" she said. She flung the locket across the hall, and it skittered to a stop at Slater's feet.

"Jessie, please," Slater tried.

"Don't worry about me, you guys," Jessie said angrily. "Just go ahead and have a blast."

She turned and rushed down the hall toward the elevator, her footsteps echoing. She turned the corner and disappeared.

Kelly took a step toward Zack. "Zack, let's go somewhere and talk."

"About what?" Zack asked stonily. "I have nothing to say to you, Kelly." He shook his head. "I can't believe you did this to me. I trusted you."

"I wanted to tell you," Kelly said, her eyes full of tears. "But I didn't want to hurt you."

"Well, congratulations," Zack said. "You did." He gave Slater an angry glance. "Thanks, *friend.*"

Zack turned on his heel and walked away. For a moment, Kelly and Slater just stood there. They heard the elevator doors open. They heard Zack and Jessie get on. There was the sound of the doors closing, and then the elevator whooshed upward again. They were gone.

Tears slowly slipped down Kelly's face. Slater bent down and picked up the silver locket. He closed his fist around it.

"Well, now they know," Kelly said faintly. "It was worse than I ever thought it would be."

"It was," Slater said hoarsely. "It was awful." He paused and turned to Kelly. "The question is, what do we do now?"

Kelly looked at him. He held up the locket.

"We could still begin," he said. "Now that they know. We can't hurt them any more than they're hurting right now. So why should we hurt ourselves more, too?"

"I don't know . . . ," Kelly said, looking away. "I don't know if I can, Slater."

Slater walked closer. He reached out and touched her hair. "I don't want to walk away from you, Kelly."

"And I don't want to walk away from you," Kelly whispered.

He drew her closer. He put an arm around her, to comfort her. She was small and fit right under his chin. He rested his cheek against her soft hair.

"So let's begin," he said.

Don't miss the next HOT novel about the
"SAVED BY THE BELL" gang

ZACK IN ACTION

Zack is in love with an exchange student from Eastern Europe. But when Screech tries his hand at investigative reporting, he discovers that Zack's new sweetie may be a spy!

Will Zack choose love over world peace? Find out in the next "Saved by the Bell" novel.